TulipTree review

FALL/WINTER 2025
issue #18

HUMOR

Mansfield, Missouri
Publisher & Editor in Chief, Jennifer Top

ISBN: 978-1-962812-06-1

www.tuliptreepub.com

Contents

GRAND PRIZE WINNER

Whitewater Bonding

Steve Holland

Risky Route

I am a moron. I know because a man once told me. Well, this man didn't actually *tell* me—he screamed it in my ear. Over and over and over. I couldn't blame him under the circumstances. He was in a life-threatening situation, and I was one-eighth to blame. And it wasn't just me he labeled a moron. His "You morons!" netted all seven of my colleagues as well. We were an eight-pack of morons, complete with matching moron helmets and moron life jackets. Thanks to our incompetence, we were moments from colliding head-on into disaster. That never would have happened, however, if I hadn't ignored the two omens.

The first omen transpired 24 hours earlier. I didn't realize it then because my four friends and I were gawking at a lonely white house 200 feet ahead. We weren't staring because the West Virginia house was beautiful. Far from it. The siding was dingy. A ripped window screen flapped in the breeze. Sticks and leaves protruded from the gutters. The porch roof sagged.

The house fascinated us because it sat 200 feet *below* us. Our jumbo green-and-white van was at a steep downward angle aimed right for it.

"I forget. Whose brilliant idea was it to travel down the gorge?" Patti sarcastically asked from her front passenger seat.

"Wait! Wait! I know this one," said Judy, sitting to my left. "The idea was your husband's."

"How was I supposed to know this road would have hairpin curves?" Fred asked, his right foot planted on the brake. "It's not like we live around here."

"It's OK, Fred," I offered. "It's not your fault the van has the turning radius of the *Titanic*. At least you found out the van has awesome seatbelts. Doesn't anyone else feel like they are defying gravity?"

"Since I can't complete the turn, I'm going to back up," Fred announced.

Fred, a policeman by trade, shifted in reverse and released the brake. The van lurched forward. Situated in the seat behind Fred's, Sheila clutched the armrests as her strawberry-blonde hair bobbed forward. Fred revved the gas, and the rear wheels spun in the loose gravel.

"Do you think the Clampetts will care if we crash into their house and stay for dinner?" I quipped.

"I hope Granny has some possum stew. Ooh, doggies!" Judy responded, her eyes fixed on the house.

"I get to sit next to Jethro," Patti added.

"Ha! Ha! I have a van full of comedians," Fred said as he stomped the gas. This time the rear wheels gripped the asphalt.

"Easy, Fred!" Patti commanded, turning to her husband. "Let's not go flying over the edge."

"How am I looking back there?" questioned Fred, gazing back at Judy and me.

"Your hair is looking good. From back here, I can't see any gray," I said. "It's all black and layered. I think you—"

"Would you mind being quiet so Fred can concentrate?" Sheila blurted in her natural Kentucky drawl.

"Sorry. By the way, Fred, I'd prefer to die while whitewater rafting tomorrow, not before."

"You've got a little bit more room," Judy interrupted, looking out the back window. "Keep coming . . . a little bit farther . . . stop."

I turned to see the plummeting drop-off a few feet away. Below was a mix of flourishing growth and decaying wilderness.

"Patti, would you toss the Wheat Thins back here?" I asked, studying the back of Patti's head.

Fred turned the wheel to the left and shifted into drive. The van jutted forward.

"You can eat at a time like this?" Sheila twanged. Sheila's hands remained fastened to the armrests.

"No, I thought I'd use the back of the box to write my will."

"Good one," Judy remarked with a chuckle. "Let me use the other side of the box when you're done."

Fred thumped the brake. The van shuddered. He shifted in reverse and faced Judy and me.

"Isn't the New River Gorge lovely in June?" Fred asked with a smirk. "I'm just happy there are no guard rails to scratch the van when we go plummeting into the woods."

The wheels again spun before Fred generously applied the gas.

"Looking good . . . Don't worry about that mime . . . a little bit more . . . far enough," I said.

Fred shifted in drive and cranked the wheel to the left. The van crept forward and cleared the corner.

"Thank God," I muttered to myself.

Because similar corners littered the zigzagging road, I thanked God several times that afternoon. The descent to a 19th-century bridge was over 850 feet. Fortunately, we reached the bridge without the van slipping off Candy Land road. Once Fred parked, we had the opportunity to escape the van, breathe fresh air, and vomit, although not necessarily in that order. We then walked on the bridge, which had been closed to traffic for 16 years—since 1977.

As I observed the swift water defy tradition and flow south to north instead of north to south, I replayed the recent experience in my mind. I realized an entrepreneur with vision could cash in on the harrowing downhill journey. The bottom of the path we just traveled was the ideal location for an underwear store. The store could be called Rock Bottom, and it would cater to everyone who had survived the trip to the bottom of New River Gorge. In the event some drivers and passengers would soil themselves on the terrifying trip downward, they could purchase "Rock Bottom Undies at Rock-Bottom Prices." Souvenir T-shirts could also be sold with catchy slogans like "I Have a Rock Bottom," "I Hit Rock Bottom in West Virginia," and "Rock Bottom Saved My Butt." A lingering odor emanating from some of the spectators on the bridge gave me the idea.

With my business idea in tow, I followed my companions inside the van. We then journeyed up the gorge unscathed. As for our unwise sightseeing expedition, Fred summarized it best.

"It was one hairy-ass ride," he declared.

Grim Discovery

I snoozed that night feeling certain the rafting adventure couldn't be more "hairy-ass" than the drive down the gorge. I slept so soundly I failed to hear Jack, one of my roommates for the trip, leave at 5 a.m. for his daily run. I assume Jack's sneakers smacked asphalt as the curly-haired band director trotted on a road alongside the railroad tracks. I also assume Jack noticed his Indiana town had the same attractions as this small West Virginia town. Gas stations, stoplight, family diner.

Everything was similar except for the dead man.

A corpse rested on its side across a train rail. Jack saw the deceased second omen but ran past as if the corpse was an empty beer can.

"I just assumed the man was a passed-out drunk," Jack said after returning from his run.

Minutes after hearing Jack's comment, I grabbed my journal, found a secluded spot, and wrote, *No more drinking with Jack. If I pass out on a railroad track, he'll leave me.*

Jack never considered the man in tattered clothing could be dead. Why would he? In Indiana the dead are displayed in funeral homes, not on railroad tracks. If the eastern and southeastern states have a bizarre funeral ritual involving railroad tracks, this ritual was never mentioned in *Deliverance*, the tell-all movie associated with eastern and southeastern states, wilderness, and whitewater. The preconceptions the rest of the US population has about the eastern and southeastern wilderness and its inhabitants come from watching *Deliverance*. Thanks to the movie, I know the wilderness in this locale is loaded with inbred rednecks who play the banjo and drawl compliments like "You gotta purty mouth, boy." The inbred rednecks also find overweight actors like Ned Beatty sexy. Nowhere in *Deliverance* did an inbred redneck place a dead person on a railroad track.

When Jack made his return trip, he spotted the whirling lights of two police cars. Jack then deduced maybe the man hadn't passed out. His suspicion was confirmed when he overheard two policemen at the scene.

"Whatcha think, Braxton?" a thin officer asked.

A short, stout officer poked the corpse's ribs with his shoe. "I think the som-bitch is dead," Braxton said. "Caleb, pull his carcass off the track."

"I'm not touchin' that dead som-bitch. He may have some contagious disease," Caleb answered. "Maybe we can git that runner to do it."

Jack accelerated and was soon past the scene. He hustled the remaining two miles to the hotel and then spilled the details.

The Rock

In my group's first 15 hours in West Virginia, five of us had barely escaped serious injury, and another member had both seen and ignored a dead man. The two incidents seemed to be warnings from above not to go whitewater rafting. Unfortunately, I failed to realize this until after the rafting trip.

Three hours after we had ignored the second omen, our eight-member group was dressing at the headquarters of Ace Whitewater. Of the eight, only one, the principal of Greensburg Community High School, possessed whitewater rafting experience. He recruited the rest of us, all foolish GCHS teachers except Fred, for his twisted rendition of faculty bonding. My principal's version differed from the average faculty bonding attempt in that his version included a greater risk of injury. At a typical teacher gathering, I had little chance of being suddenly catapulted from my seat and sent head-first into a boulder. Being seriously injured, however, was a possibility with whitewater bonding.

The outfitter provided us with life jackets, plastic helmets, and optional wetsuits. Since I hate being cold, I crammed myself into a snug wetsuit. It was like stuffing a sausage casing. After putting on the rest of my gear, I examined myself in a mirror. I was the opposite of a rugged outdoorsman. I knew instantly I was destined to be a cover boy for a nature magazine with a nerdy title, something like *Outdoor Geek*. A tight chin strap clamped my blue helmet to my head like a crown on an acorn. Just below the helmet, my enormous glasses treated my weak nose like a slide. My blue jacket and blue and yellow life preserver hid my bony arms and lean midsection, but when it came to below my waist, there was no mistaking my lack of weight. The tight, black wetsuit made me appear as if I had pipe cleaners instead of legs. I wore a pair of beat-up, white high tops to complete my ensemble. I had transformed into *July Geek 1993*.

With paddles in hand, my fellow rafters and I boarded a former school bus and traveled down a narrow path that led to the river. When I looked out my window, I noticed the bus was traveling only five feet from the side of another plummeting drop-off. I instantly recalled the previous day's harrowing downhill journey. So did another bus passenger.

"John, you won't believe this! Yesterday Wilma and me saw some dumbass driving a huge green and white van down the road to the old bridge!" a man bellowed from the rear of the bus. "You know the road, the one only small vehicles use. What the hell was that dumbass thinkin'?"

The man earned chuckles while the dumbass in question sat silently in front of me with his wife. His dumbass passengers, including me, also remained silent.

After reaching the bottom, we trickled from the bus and gathered around Tom, our trip leader. Tom's rugged brown and gray beard made it clear he was the most experienced of the trip's four guides.

"The river is at a springtime water level," Tom announced. "That means you're in for one helluva ride!"

I appreciated having an enthusiastic leader, but I would have preferred a ride that wasn't associated with Hell. I wanted either a heavenly ride, a so-so ride, or the senior citizens' special. "One helluva ride" sounded too chaotic.

The other three guides gathered their groups, piled into their self-bailing blue rafts, and paddled north. My seven Greensburg colleagues, Tom, and a female guide-in-training then climbed aboard our raft. Five people sat on each side of the raft. I was the fourth person on the right side. Because there were no seats, we sat on the sides of the raft while we each wedged a foot underneath the side for an anchor. Tom was behind me in a white helmet, and to his left was the guide-in-training.

"What a glorious day for rafting!" Tom exclaimed as we paddled away from shore. "We will be traveling thirteen miles today, and we will end up near the New River Gorge Bridge, the world's largest single-arch steel span bridge. It is over three thousand feet long. The bridge is truly a magnificent site."

The ride started smooth and easy. Our paddles methodically sliced into the rippling current. We were surrounded on both sides by walls of wilderness. A clear sky above and gurgling water beneath completed the frame. For the time being, the trip was perfect.

The perfect trip was ruined 20 minutes later when I witnessed screaming people from the other rafts jumping off a miniature cliff. They plunged into the river, and water shot upward.

“That’s Jump Rock,” Tom explained. “Tradition dictates we stop there so you can all jump. You will then swim downstream to the raft.”

This news filled me with apprehension. Maybe after we finished jumping off the feebly named rock, we could head-butt sugar maple trees or take turns dodging flaming arrows. I had no desire to leap off Jump Rock, Kid Rock, or any rock, for that matter. I was afraid of heights. Jump Rock appeared to have a 15-foot drop, and no Rock Bottom underwear store was nearby in case of emergency.

Tom made jumping sound optional, but it wasn’t, not when everyone else was jumping. If I failed to jump, I would be silently branded a 30-year-old nerd. Although I looked the part, I disliked the label. Fortunately, I had no intention of wimping out. I live by the credo “I’ll try anything once,” and this has occasionally forced me to confront my fear of heights. This includes the time I gazed at New York City’s magnificent panorama from an Empire State Building outside observation deck. I stood 1,211 feet from the ground and 10 feet from the safety wall. Many spectators were next to the safety wall, but I was close enough. Moving closer and throwing up were not necessary.

I nervously waited on the top of the massive rock while rafters took turns running to the edge and jumping. Three people from my raft had already jumped when Patti dashed to the edge and suddenly stopped. She looked down, panicked, and turned around for another 20-foot sprint down the runway. I knew if I thought too long about the jump, I would also retreat.

As soon as Patti was clear, I took off running. I came to the ledge, pushed off with my right foot . . . and slipped. Luckily, I had enough momentum to clear the edge. I was airborne. My arms and legs tingled and scrambled eggs and bacon surged into my throat. I splashed down and flapped my arms like a bird to propel to the surface. I then swam to the raft, feeling fortunate I hadn’t whacked myself on the cliff’s edge.

The next person wasn’t so lucky.

Judy, a short, heavy-set art teacher, was the unlucky participant. The 51-year-old educator scooted down the runway and, like me, slipped near the ledge. Unlike me, she fell, landed on her butt, and bounced off the cliff's edge like a rubber ball. Judy completed her amazing routine by landing belly-first in the frigid water. Her performance wasn't graceful, but it was entertaining. I was later able to enjoy the feat because an Ace Whitewater employee videotaped the spectacle. Fred purchased the video that highlighted the day's adventure. Soon after, Fred repeatedly showed Judy's exploit on the van's TV/VCR. He even enhanced Judy's routine by using the *reverse* button. Judy was now able to bounce off the cliff, smack the water, submerge, and then miraculously shoot upward from the water like a missile and return to the cliff's edge. She performed her painful routine again and again, never tiring. Judy's acrobatic performance received rave reviews from an appreciative, laughing audience.

Man Overboard

After the Jump Rock initiation, my next big scare came in the early afternoon. By that point we had five rapids under our belts, and the sixth was visible ahead. We knew the routine. A rapid followed a stretch of calm water. We bounced for 30 seconds of terror, and then we returned to tranquility. The ride was an adrenaline junkie's dream, but I hated it. If the rapids could have been removed from the whitewater rafting trip, I would have enjoyed myself. Instead, I was dripping and scared, but I tried to focus on the positive—I wasn't lying dead on a railroad track.

As we approached the rapid, the current's speed increased. The rushing waters ahead hissed like radio static. The raft swayed as we approached the frothing waves. I dug my squeaking right sneaker under the raft's side and scooted my butt a couple inches to the left. The waves grew larger and more powerful. We rocked up and down. When the front of the raft rose, the rear dipped. When the front dipped, I and the other rear mates rose. I was riding nature's version of a roller coaster.

Some of the other crew members laughed and yelled in delight, but I didn't. My bulging eyes and death grip on my paddle spoke for me. They screamed, "I'M TERRIFIED!"

The high speed and constant rocking made the experience nerve-racking. Having my pain-dispensing dental hygienist clean my teeth was more fun. At one point, the front of our raft shot upward and rammed a wall of water that soaked the front foursome. We all kept paddling, but I was faster than everyone else. My arms whirled. I paddled like a mallard on speed because I was horrified.

Powerful waves smacked me in the face as we continued our downward run. I was too busy paddling in hyper-drive to care. I was as frightened as a mouse in the jaws of a python.

My body jiggled as the waves continued their assault. Crashing waves attacked from all sides. The ride was no longer a roller coaster. We were now caught in nature's washing machine. The barrage of waves sounded like Niagara Falls.

I was only a novice, but I thought the shocks on our raft sucked. Before we attacked the next rapid, we needed to trade our raft for a smoother-riding model. Hopefully, a Mercedes-Benz or Rolls-Royce raft dealership was waiting around the next bend.

As for our jarring ride, it reminded me of a motion simulation theater I once had endured in Disneyland. I watched a four-and-a-half-minute movie called *Star Tours*, and I felt as if I was aboard a spaceship dodging asteroids. The combination of special effects and a rocking theater had the children near me cackling and cheering. I didn't know what was so damn amusing. Were they blind? Our little theater was going to smash into an asteroid! Those kids were lucky I didn't bring my light saber.

Like *Star Tours*, the rapid provided enough terror to make me cower like a frightened cocker spaniel. Bent over, I continued paddling until a wave hammered the rear left side of the raft. The impact jolted me from my seat. My head and shoulders dangled over the side, but my anchored right foot saved me from going overboard. I pulled myself up just as another wave rocked the rear of the raft. This time Fred sailed overboard. I had the perfect view because Fred had been paddling in front of me. The last thing I saw was Fred's Vietnam-issued jungle boots.

"These babies will keep me anchored," Fred had gloated earlier about his black combat boots with the steel-reinforced soles.

Anchored to the bottom of the river was probably not what Fred had in mind.

Luckily, Fred grabbed the rope on the side of the raft before that could happen. He kept his head above the foaming water, and his legs disappeared underneath the raft. The waves mellowed moments later.

"Pull him in," Tom ordered.

Sheila responded. Since she sat across from Fred, Sheila was responsible for grabbing the 45-year-old police officer by the shoulders of his life jacket, falling backward, and pulling Fred from the water. Sheila tugged on the 6'4", 210-pound Vietnam War veteran. Fred's head rose momentarily above the raft before Sheila groaned and released her grip. Fred splashed into his original position.

"Pull him in," Tom repeated.

My fellow crew members and I stopped paddling to watch the show. Fred's undersized savior yanked and duplicated her prior performance. Fred's head resembled a blue bobber. Considering the weight mismatch, I thought Fred was a goner. Sheila had a better chance of pulling Excalibur from a stone farther down the river.

Seeing Fred's predicament caused me to gaze across the raft at Judy. I didn't like my survival chances if I sailed overboard, particularly if Judy had peeked at my will on the Wheat Thins box. Willing Judy my *Christmas with the Brady Bunch* music CD may have been a bad decision.

"You know what to do," Tom would tell Judy after I would sail overboard.

"I certainly do," Judy would mutter to herself. She then would grab my shoulder straps and lower her head near mine.

"All I get is a lousy Brady Bunch CD?" she would whisper, her bangs resting near her eyes.

"It was a joke."

"Bad choice, funny man," Judy would whisper as she would pry my fingers from the rope. After loosening my last finger, Judy would push my face from the raft and say, "I'm sorry, Tom, but Steve didn't make it."

"Get Fred in this raft!" Tom yelled, snapping me back to reality.

The current's speed increased, and the hiss of radio static signaled we were already approaching the next rapid.

"Come on! You've got to get him in now!" Tom hollered. "Why has everyone else stopped paddling? Paddle!"

I saw the churning waves ahead and sank my paddle in the water. Sheila grimaced and tugged on Fred's right shoulder, while Patti, who had turned around, yanked on Fred's left shoulder.

"GET HIM IN! GET HIM IN!" Tom screamed.

Fred's midsection rose from the water. Sheila and Patti yanked as Fred seized the side of the raft and pulled his legs from the river. He then flopped into the raft.

"PADDLE!" Tom ordered.

Sheila, Patti, and Fred sprang into their spots, but it was too late. Because we had stopped paddling to say a premature farewell to Fred, we were out of position for entering the next rapid. Angry waves attacked from all sides and shoved the raft like driftwood. The roaring water was deafening. We paddled fiercely but in vain.

"YOU MORONS!" Tom yelled. "YOU MORONS! YOU MORONS!"

I was glad I wasn't the only one panicking. I would have preferred, however, that my panic-stricken partner was a crew member and not our guide. I could have also done without the name-calling. Calling a group of educators *morons* was like me screaming, "THIS RAFTING TRIP IS AWESOME! I LOVED THE PART WHEN FRED ALMOST DIED!"

The raft continued to rock back and forth, and water invaded all sides. An avalanche of waves knocked us from our course, and we momentarily floated sideways. A sudden drop of water then whipped us back in the right direction. Although I was a rafting rookie, I didn't need Tom to tell me we were in over our heads. This had to be a Class V rapid. Considering rapids range from the easy Class I to the foolish-to-attempt Class VI, this rapid had Class V written on each violent, incoming wave.

To make matters even more outlandish, our raft suddenly decided to take a breather. In the middle of all that chaos, our raft drifted and bizarrely parked atop a ramp-shaped boulder protruding in the middle of the river. We were now the inflatable cherry resting on the top of a whitewater sundae. The boulder we were currently sunning ourselves on would have been the perfect launching pad for a jet-propelled trout hoping to set a daredevil jump record. What I liked about the boulder, though, was that it elevated us above the violently swirling whitewater.

I sat silently as I tried to wrap my head around what just happened. We had run aground, or more appropriately, "run aboulder," in the middle of a raging river. Wow! Our initial looks of bewilderment were now replaced by smiles. We were saved!

This tranquility, however, was short-lived. After a joyous 20 seconds of being stationary, the raft began to slide backward down the boulder.

"Oh, shit," Fred said just loud enough for me to hear.

"NOOOO!" I yelled.

We weren't saved. It was merely halftime, and the second half was moments from beginning.

Once the entire raft returned to the water, we spun in circles. At this point, we were completely out of control. I was overcome with a feeling of helplessness, the same sense of helplessness drivers feel when their vehicles slide on ice at high speeds. Even when we stopped spinning, the rocking waters were almost unbearable.

Scared and soaked, I concentrated on making invisible circles with my arms. When my paddling speed suddenly increased, I peered over the side of the raft. A massive whirlpool twirled in the middle of the river. The left side of the raft sat on the edge of the swirl, and my side of the raft hung over the edge. We were moments away from being flushed down a giant toilet bowl like a batch of turds.

I was able to paddle faster because my paddle wasn't touching water. This discovery would have stopped an ordinary person from paddling, but not me. I continued paddling the air. I also decided against updating my fellow turds on our situation.

Amazingly, we avoided being flushed, and my side of the raft returned to sit on churning waters. Twenty seconds later the waves finally dissipated.

We survived but were drained both physically and emotionally. That much was apparent as we silently paddled to the next rapid. A minute passed before I heard Tom interrupt the rhythmic sound of paddles pushing water.

"I was seconds from telling everyone to jump," Tom quietly confessed to the guide-in-training.

You moron, I thought. *Keep thoughts like that to yourself.*

Memory Loss

We successfully navigated over 20 rapids that day, but the rapid I still recall best is the one that tried to kill us. Those few minutes of terror defined the trip for me. Now when people ask me about the time I went whitewater rafting in West Virginia, I reply, "Oh, you mean the time I almost got sucked in a whirlpool and died."

Oddly, time has had the opposite effect on my fellow travelers. When they regale others of our adventure, they apparently remember only the joyous bits because they say the trip was great fun. They mention nothing about the satanic rapid. It is as if that entire incident never happened.

"You heard our rafting trip was dangerous?" one of them might reply to an inquisitive friend. "Ridiculous. It was child's play. Have you ever ridden a lazy river at a water park? It was like that."

Some of my fellow travelers have even said they would like to go whitewater rafting again someday.

Without me, that's for sure.

Whiskey

Allan M. Heller

I pushed open the swinging doors and took a glance at my surroundings as I strolled into the Fanfare Saloon in Trope, Wyoming. Funny name for a town, I thought. Searching for a friendly face, I saw that surly neutrality would have to suffice, and bellying up to the bar, settled on a spot near where three ranch hands had staked their claim. They stood to my right, gruffly grousing about their rancid libations. The guy next to me shot me a suspicious glance, then returned to his conversation.

The bartender approached.

"Whiskey," I said.

With deft hands he snatched up a shot glass and placed it in front of me, then quickly filled it to the brim, not spilling a drop of the golden liquid.

"Two bits," he informed me.

I set a quarter on the counter.

Clearing my throat, I said, "Do you serve anything here besides whiskey?"

"Nope."

"So, would I be correct in assuming that for the customer to actually pick his poison would be superfluous?" I asked.

This drew the attention, as well as the ire, of the aforementioned man to my right.

"Why do you ask stupid questions, mister?" he snapped.

Momentarily I was taken aback, but quickly composed myself, launching yet another inquiry, this time at him.

"Why are you so damn ugly?" Not my most sophisticated comeback, but there was no sense blunting my rapier wit on this dullard.

Pushing himself away from the bar, he drew himself to his full height—an impressive five foot six—and faced me. He was muscular, but not excessively, and his florid complexion was augmented by a thick red beard and hair to match. His nose was like a flattened tomato. His sharp blue eyes seethed contempt.

Straightening his hat, he growled, "You take that back."

The bartender saw fit to intervene. Taking a shotgun from under the bar, he cocked the weapon in full view of everyone.

"Hobart, I don't want no trouble from you or anybody else. So just calm down." Hobart stood down, for the moment, and I figured that if his mother had named him "Enoch" instead, that would have given him the extra belligerence needed to fuel an altercation.

I gulped my whiskey, ordered another, and sent it down the hatch, as well. The three patrons to my right had been accurate in their assessment of the refreshments, but after a third dose, I wasn't concerned with taste. The din of drinkers and gamblers had grown considerably louder since my entrance, while the piano player blithely hammered out "Goodbye, Liza Jane." I ordered a fourth shot.

I grinned at the bartender. "Whiskey." He didn't return the grin.

Three or four members of the fairer sex strolled among the throng of revelers. One of the ladies found her way to me, and slipping her arm around my shoulder, cooed, "Hey there, handsome. Wanna go upstairs?"

I blinked hard, my eyes bone dry and my vision slightly blurry. "Heck. I don't know," I slurred. I'd already taken five shots of whiskey at this point, and wasn't confident to walk a straight line, let alone to, well . . .

But that was a decision that I didn't have to make, for at that moment, the swinging doors parted to admit a frightful trio of darkly dressed, unshaven desperadoes brandishing ponderous pistols. How did I know that they were "desperadoes?" I could just tell (plus the fact that they wore black hats).

The clamor instantly subsided. The piano stopped midway through "Beautiful Dreamer." Everyone—yes, everyone—looked in the direction of the menacing threesome.

The leader spoke up.

"What the hell are you all lookin' at?" he barked at the entire ensemble.

I personally didn't know what to say, but I spoke anyway. Probably the alcohol talking.

"Sir, I believe that they are looking at you."

His head jerked toward me. "Mister, don't you know what a rhetorical question is?"

Pleasantly surprised at his choice of vocabulary, I replied, "Yes, I do." He stomped his way to the bar, and holstered his gun.

"I need a drink," he mused, staring at the myriad bottles lined up along the base of the wall mirror. "Hmm."

Finally he settled on something.

"Whiskey," he grunted.

Hands shaking, the bartender served him. The stranger took a delicate sip. Before anyone knew what was going on, he shot a mean glance at one of the card players, who had allowed an audible chuckle to escape his lips. This ratcheted up to a full-blown guffaw.

"I'm sorry," the doomed gambler gasped through giggles. "I never seen anyone drink whiskey like they was sippin' lemonade!"

The outlaw's face curled into an icy snarl, at which point he drew his gun with amazing alacrity and obliterated the hapless chortler.

One of the men seated at the table with the dearly departed gave a low whistle.

"Amazing," he gasped.

This time the gunslinger grinned. "Impressed with my skill?"

"No," the gambler replied. "You shot him clean in the heart, and there's no blood!"

"Never is," the killer said.

The unmistakable squeaking of the saloon's swinging doors sounded again, admitting two men wearing gun belts, leather vests, and silver stars pinned on the chest.

"Hello, Sheriff Wilson. Deputy Drake," the gunman said, his tone without rancor or threat.

"Larry, I'm takin' you in," the sheriff advised him.

"I don't think so, Sheriff," Larry replied.

The packed bar cleared out in 30 seconds. Some of them even dashed for the back exit, breaking the locked door into splinters. I stood rooted to my spot, unable to move. What was the matter with me?

Larry showed no fear. In a flashbang of deadly dueling, he and his two cronies aimed their pistols at the pair of lawmen and fired. Sheriff Wilson and Deputy Drake managed to draw their guns, but were too late, going down in a hail of lead. While the villains were blazing away, I noticed that the lesser two thugs kept waving their free hands over the barrel of their guns and tapping the hammer with their palm after each shot. This annoyed Larry.

"Why do you morons keep fanning your guns? These are Colt .45 double-action revolvers. You don't need to cock them after every shot."

"But they always do that in Westerns," one of his dim-witted minions replied.

Larry grimaced. "What Westerns?"

"I dunno."

While the outlaws were distracted, I decided to surreptitiously effect an escape. This seemed the safest course of action. Also, the five shots of whiskey had finally caught up with me, necessitating a trip to the outhouse. Four feet separated me from the familiar swinging doors when Larry called out, “Where do you think you’re going?”

“I— I need to use the john,” I stammered.

Larry aimed his Colt directly at my forehead. “Do you?”

I gulped. “Actually, not anymore.”

Waving his gun playfully, he informed me, “Jed and Ted and I can’t let you leave, Mister . . . ?”

“Walker,” I supplied. “Johnnie Walker.”

“Mr. Walker. Nothing personal, but you’re a witness to the killing of two lawmen. You could have left when everybody else did. Why didn’t you?”

“I’ll be asking that question for the rest of my life,” I replied.

“That ain’t gonna be too long,” said Jed. Or maybe it was Ted.

“Tell you what, though,” said Larry. “Since I’m a sporting gentleman, I’m going to give you a fighting chance.” He motioned to one of his cronies. “Ted, bring Sheriff Wilson’s gun over here.”

“It’s Jed, boss,” he replied.

Larry snorted. “Whatever. Bring me his gun.”

Jed complied. Examining the pistol, Larry said, “Still has three bullets. And there are three of us.”

I wish that I could say that I started sweating bullets, which would have been helpful, but instead I started sweating like anybody else.

“I’m still outnumbered,” I protested weakly.

To my utter surprise, Larry aimed and fired the late sheriff’s pistol, first at Jed, and then at Ted. Or maybe it was Ted, and then Jed. Regardless, both slumped to the floor dead.

I gasped. “Jed and Ted are dead,” I said. “And there’s no blood.”

“I never could tell them apart,” Larry remarked. He then tossed the sheriff’s gun to me.

“Now we’re even,” he said. “Or close enough. Let’s step outside, Mr. Walker. I’m calling you out.”

As he exited, he shouted over his shoulder. “If you don’t come out in five minutes, I’m coming back in for you.”

I was totally devoid of any plan or strategy. I had a gun with one bullet, and a more-than-competent killer waiting for me out in the street. I staggered behind the bar to see if there was anything that would give me a little edge. Something like . . . a Gatling gun. Okay, not really. Then I had an idea.

I stumbled out into the brisk, sunny February afternoon, the sun glare searing my eyes. There he was, waiting, 30 feet from me, his gun still holstered. I was wearing the sheriff's leather vest, which was too large for me, but perfect for what I needed. Booming, dramatic music thundered from the sky, so loud that I could hardly hear anything else.

Doing my best to appear menacing, I gripped the butt of the gun firmly and met Larry's stare. "Well, well, well," he taunted me. "Looks like we have a new sheriff in town. You know how this works, Mr. Walker?"

"What?" I shouted over the music.

"I said, do you know how this works?" Larry shouted in return.

I nodded.

"Fine," Larry said. "On the count of three. One, two—"

I raised my gun and fired, not daring to wait until three. Simultaneously I felt like a hammer slammed into my chest, knocking me down. I lay there for a few minutes, too sore and too stunned to move. I heard many voices gathering in the background, getting closer and clearer. The overhead orchestral accompaniment had subsided.

Townspeople crowded me, asking me if I was all right, and telling me what a hero I was for gunning down Lethal Larry Largo. I pulled myself into a sitting position and asked, "Where is he?"

A man in the crowd pointed to where Larry lay, flat on his back and dead in the dust. Taking off the sheriff's leather vest, I removed the silver serving platter that had stopped a bullet.

"I shot him," I said, amazed.

Yes, I did, several of the townspeople assured me. They helped me to my feet and carried me back into the Fanfare.

"How about a drink to celebrate, Sheriff?"

"Sheriff?" I said. Then I thought, why not?

Standing up at the counter, I saw that the bartender was back in his typical spot. Someone shouted, "A drink for Sheriff . . . ?"

"Walker," I said.

The bartender asked me, "What'll it be, Sheriff Walker?"

I grinned. "Do you really need to ask?"

Diva Pariah

Shauna Hicks

Imagine getting fired from the job of your dreams and on your last day, you get stuck in a crowded elevator made up entirely of your boss and coworkers. That's the closest I can come to describing my two days at sea after being fired on a cruise ship. The cruise line shall remain nameless, but let's just say I was a *Celebrity* vocalist, and I had bombed terribly, excruciatingly, and had No! Idea! Why!

I found out I had tanked the next day when I read this email from my agent: "Hi— According to the cruise director, there have been many complaints. They are releasing you from your contract and are requesting that you disembark in San Juan on Monday. Is everything okay? Are you having vocal problems?"

Good thing I had used the head before heading to check email. My mind morphed into a stampede of rabid cattle. What happened? I thought I had killed the night before, but clearly I had bombed! Flashes of me on stage before a packed house! Roughly a thousand people in tuxes and gowns on that grand night! Me, smiling! Strutting! Killing it on the formidable formal night. And then? Formalities had been followed. I had been formally requested to leave the ship.

"Are you having vocal problems?"

I managed a stiff upper lip, dashed off an email to my agent apologizing for putting her in this position. *Voice felt fine*. I would *look into things*. Would *circle back*. I logged off, then wandered out of that computer room in a mortified daze, desperate to find a staff member to help me solve the mystery of what I'd done on stage last night. Of course, I wanted to avoid passengers. Walking to breakfast earlier in the day, I now understood why person after person looked away upon seeing me. I ate breakfast in that bustling cafe alone. No one approached. No one said,

"Good show last night! We really enjoyed it! Will you be performing again?"

I had become a Diva Pariah, stuck at sea with the people who had put my head on a spike. But why? Thankfully, dinner was a few hours away, and the ship was quite empty on this gentle, rolling day at sea. Most of my audience was likely napping in their staterooms.

Walking with my head low to the fore of the ship, I passed the casino and got lucky. No one noticed me. When I turned the corner I spotted Silvio, my bass player, sitting alone in the Coffee Cafe with a book, a croissant, and a cappuccino. What a nice private moment for him . . . until I plopped myself down across from him with the vibe of a shipwrecked woman flagging down a plane. As for Silvio? His vibe brought to mind a cat that had just fallen into a bathtub. His big brown eyes were wide with panic and could not meet mine. He crouched over and he kept shaking his head while muttering,

No, no, no, no, no.

Oh my! It was worse than I'd thought! I attempted some chumminess.

Hey . . . It's okay . . . I just wanna talk.

But Silvio wasn't having it. He was like the cool kid in junior high, suffering the invasion of his lunch table by the zitty kid who'd yet to discover deodorant.

No, no . . . I don't want to talk to you, he said tersely.

To my surprise, I begged,

Silvio, please! What's going on?

He shook his head, so I added,

Hey, they've already fired me. Okay? So really. I just need to know what happened.

This seemed to settle him a bit.

You really *don't know?*

No! I really *don't.*

He opened his mouth, started to speak, then shook his head.

No, I can't, he said.

I was just short of pounding my head repeatedly on his table.

Please, Silvio! Please, I'm dying here!

It was strangely fascinating to witness him wince as if I'd just turned screws attached to his scrotum.

Pitch, he whispered.

Bolts of dread and panic surged through me. They were so unbearable, I attempted to stomp them out with denial.

Pitch! Huh? Really? Well, that's never *been a problem for me before. How bad was it?*

BAD, he confirmed firmly.

Reeling, I felt like an unprepared court-ordered public defender talking out of her ass.

Huh . . . Where exactly?

Silvio reacted as if I'd tasered him.

EVERYWHERE! ALL OF IT! THE ENTIRE SHOW!

And then with brutal emphasis he said softly,

And "People."

Oh no. My finale. Streisand's "People." I'd *murdered* "People."

What about it? I asked.

But I didn't really want to know. He still couldn't look at me. He just shook his twenty-something head full of thick brown hair and moaned as if his appendix was bursting and there was no ambulance in sight.

"People." "People" was the worst . . . *So bad. So, SO bad.*

I thanked poor Silvio with a new understanding that he'd been thoroughly tarred with my brush. If the band were a football team, I was the star halfback who'd repeatedly spiked the ball after scoring multiple touchdowns in the wrong end zone! *Worse!* I'd done obnoxious VICTORY dances in the wrong end zone! Again and again!

It all came rushing back to me in a strobe light frenzy. Last night? I had *celebrated* through the entire show! Feeling my own private, euphoric joy! Why? Because back on land? Weeks before boarding that ship? I'd been *limping*. Sharp pain in my right knee that would have had me hobbling through "These Boots Are Made for Walking" like Quasimodo in sequins. Yes, back on land with this headliner contract looming, I had dark visions of a packed formal night filled with retired married couples all whispering to each other,

"Is it my imagination? Or is she *limping*?"

"Yeah, hon. I think you're right. That woman is *definitely* limping? Oh *poor* thing, I hope she's okay. It *hurts* just watching her. Let's sneak out to the casino when she's not lookin'.

And so, last night, after weeks of vigorous physical therapy, I was beyond relieved to be spared that dreaded scenario! Such the joy to be strutting, strolling, and parading confidently with nary a thought of the ring in my ear . . . a new sound that had taken up residence in my skull months earlier. Ever since, music had sounded a bit off. But what of it? I'd always viewed my voice as a winning slot machine with dinging bells and cascading coins. The bells were now out of key, but I'd thought I'd be fine. Nothing to worry about, but I *was* worried about my knee, and I took care of it. Now, I felt like a figure skater with a strange psychological tick. Falling over and over again, oblivious but obvious to everyone else. I'm skating along, smiling, gesturing happily, spreading my arms victoriously, and splatting on my triple axles, but bouncing up like I'd just nailed it!

"Look at me! Aren't I somethin'?!"

I was something all right. A Norma Desmond believing the camera is moving in for her close-up, smiling confidently in the spotlight, and wrapped in a straightjacket.

The other headliner was Mark, a comic. He had a lot to say, and his words were like honey on my soul.

I just thought you were having trouble hearing the monitors, but nobody walked out, right? You held 'em. They stayed.

He was right. They had stayed in vague disbelief. A rubber-necking fascination.

Mark went on,

And, hey, everyone gets fired in show business. It's a rite of passage. Take me! If I had a dollar for every time I got fired, I could buy a car. Not a nice *car, but a car.*

And he pointed out something that had not occurred to me.

This is not about your talent. You have an injury. *Now, go talk to the cruise director and apologize for putting him this position and let him know that this is not by any means an indication of who you are as a talent. This is a* medical *condition you were not aware of. You'll take care of it, and hope he'll give you another shot.*

I was old enough to be that cruise director's mother . . . in some states, his grandmother. When I knocked on his door, he morphed into a doppelgänger of Silvio. Looking down at his desk. Nodding uncomfortably. But could I blame him? He'd stepped out on formal night and told them,

Ladies and Gentlemen! You're in for a treat! Direct from Broadway! Pah-LEASE put your hands together FOR . . . a delusional woman singing off key.

How'd it go? Mark asked.

Not great. He hates me. Shades of Silvio.

Well, shake it off, he said. *He's scared. He's just a kid.*

Yeah . . . you're right. Thanks. Well, I'm gonna go crawl under the rock that is my stateroom.

You do that. Take it easy and get some sleep, Mark said.

And I did. Eventually. Because Mark was right. My pitch had been hijacked and that could be fixed. As for last night? What had I done *really*? Sure, I'd murdered "People," but it's not like I *murdered* people.

Great Expectations

David Margolis

Spring finally arrived, and with it, the intoxicating scent of the wild honeysuckle overgrowing my yard. Rabbits mated and multiplied, tadpoles swarmed on the pool cover, and the redbud tree bloomed magnificently with the branches that were still alive. It was at that exact moment that the seed of creativity germinated in my mind. The tiny speck of genius that would grow to an epic masterpiece, the oeuvre of my writing career.

However, spring turned into summer, followed by a disappointing fall, which preceded a bonkers winter. This might lead one to suspect a hint of procrastination, but nothing could be further from the truth. Thoughts and ideas continued to bubble in my brain, waiting for the right time to burst forth. And yes, today is the day that I put my pen to paper.

The opening lines will describe a dashing, charismatic man who has his way with the ladies, someone in the mold of a Clark Gable or a George Clooney, someone like myself. I have in mind a murder mystery in the Agatha Christie style, but with the literary thrust of a William Faulkner. I haven't completely ruled out a love affair between a retired soldier of fortune and an elderly wench.

On the other hand, I could write a metaphysical poem about good and evil and God, a modern-day *Paradise Lost*. And like John Milton, I'll wake every morning dictating the next ten pages that have come to me in my nightly dream. The Tree of Knowledge might even float down from heaven and take the form of my redbud in its prime. It might have a sonorous voice akin to the burning bush of the Old Testament, or perhaps the mobility of the Birnam Wood of *Macbeth*.

Time is of the essence, let's begin! I had written a page a few months ago, actually more of an outline, at least I had my name on the paper with the title "Red Buddy." But sadly—on that very same day—I hurt my back putting my legs up the wall in yoga class. I was laid up for a few months and was forced to curtail my practice. As anyone can tell you, it's impossible to have writing thoughts if you're not meditating in Shavasana, never mind the fact that it was impossible to plonk down into my well-worn writing chair. Last month, I purchased an ergonomic rocker and refurbished my study with acoustic panels. I'm one of those people that can't get anything done unless there's complete silence—a pin dropping can throw off my collection of meaningful phrases.

I'm looking at the fonts available on my Microsoft Word. I'd like to choose one that captures the mood of the piece. I toy with Arial Rounded MT Bold, before considering the playful Bahnschrift Light Condensed, or even Bahnschrift Light Semi Condensed. After pondering the more robust Copperplate Gothic Bold, I finally settle on Baskerville Old Face, but I'll be certain to check the submission requirements with Harper's before I make a final decision.

I'll need to change the battery in my Logitech mouse. There'll be plenty of cheese to ingest today. I inspect the printer for paper and discover there's only twelve sheets in the bin. I check my phone for the best prices, but end up scrolling the latest news. I try to thwart a resulting anxiety attack with deep breathing exercises and muscle relaxation. I put in a phone call to my therapist.

Suddenly, there's the distinct sizzle of a synapse connection, cloaked in the form of an idea. I'm prepared to write at least five thousand words this morning, after I take a short walk to prevent my head from exploding. It's a chilly March morning with a cloudy sky. I consider walking my dog, an obese dachshund, who could use the exercise, but then again, she doesn't enjoy the company of other dogs or people, and she tends to bite. She gives me that droopy look, and I decide to include her on my journey.

I keep my head down, my eyes fixed on the uninspiring cement of the cracked sidewalk, partially covered by the gray and brown leaves of a retreating winter. I visit a nearby pond, which was once infested with summer algae and a small army of obstreperous geese, but now is deathly still. A putrid smell of nearby trash bins lingers in the air. Thoreau couldn't have composed a grocery list after encountering such a body of water.

I intrepidly push on, trying not to forget the thoughts that I once remembered. Random words fill the void: alliterations such as Tommy Tuberville, and funky verbs like thump, babble, gurgle, and clunk. Fortunately, there are some resolute metaphors in the mix.

For many years, I've imagined a dialogue between my redbud in its prime, and an ash tree that cohabitated nearby. Sadly, this tree succumbed to ash borer several years ago, but was the inspiration for a previous story, "Kiss My Ash," that almost appeared in *The New Yorker*. They thanked me for submitting my work, so they must have loved it. But now that the ash has expired, I intend to write a conversation between the Japanese maple and a nearby dogwood, in English of course, with some derisive laughter from a nearby spruce, or maybe just a wistful sigh. I can't think of what they'll exactly say to each other, but they won't be holding hands, that's for sure.

I notice a rumbling in my tummy, approaching almost cramp-like intensity, but not quite. I received a letter six months ago to have a repeat colonoscopy, but I was so busy contemplating my story and ministering to my lumbar spine that I haven't followed up. I'm interrupted by the dachshund snoring at my feet. Overweight dogs snore just like humans.

My gut discomfort eases with a hearty belch and a small fart. In my excitement, I've forgotten about breakfast. I begin to toast a whole wheat bagel. I'd prefer an onion and garlic flavor, but a spicy variety might be too irritating for my finicky esophagus. The bell on the toaster rings. I place my crusty bagel on my Dump Trump plastic souvenir plate that I purchased in 2016. The bagel is stale, the butter's too hard, and the cream cheese is cheddar jalapeno. I put the butter in the microwave and open a new tub of plain cream cheese, but then the butter's too soft, the cream cheese is too bland, and the coffee is too cold. I check the refrigerator. The eggs have expired and the bacon's not kosher. I decide to eliminate the rabbinical student as the protagonist of my story.

I drive to Walgreens for a bottle of Pepto-Bismol and a colorful assortment of Tums, just in case the tranquility of my gut is temporary. While I'm there, I purchase some trail mix that's on sale for $1.99. There's nothing better than some munchies when one is writing something significant. Next door is an Office Depot. I buy computer paper and an extra-large ink cartridge for all the printing that I plan to do. I select an ergonomic mouse to match my ergonomic chair, then look at some writing desks and a reading lamp. Maybe I'll need a laptop to compose my story. I'll be able to write in my backyard while viewing nature's beauty. I buy a spiral notebook to corral any stray thoughts that might crop up during my writing adventure.

I stop at Trader Joe's to procure a bag of prunes and a loaf of high-fiber bread. At Costco, I pick up a nine-pound brisket for two, three dozen apples, and 36 pencils to edit my writing. I visit Pooch Paradise to buy doggie treats and a large bag of low-calorie chow. I decide to visit a tree nursery. I purchase a crab apple sapling and a jocular juniper. I arrive home and begin preparations to write. I'm now face to face with the computer, the screen as white as the blinding snow of an arctic blizzard before global warming.

I browse the Amazon website and order three packages of computer paper that are cheaper than the ones I bought at Office Depot. I'll return the paper this afternoon. I contemplate walking there —it's only three miles. On the way, I might invent some clever idioms or maybe a simple simile, but probably not. I look at my watch; it's almost time for lunch.

Joan's Stone on Loan

Lyss Buchthal

IN MY DEFENSE, how else was I going to get his number?

Picture this: Thursday evening, five p.m., LA traffic, the intersection of Pico and La Cienega. You see the most *beautiful* man you have ever seen in your life driving the car in front of you. Not even his whole face, just a sliver—brown eye, freckled skin, angular cheekbone, deep-set brow. You're one green light away from the world's worst missed connection: What would you do?

It was *supposed* to be gentle. A love-tap, really.

A silly little rear-end incident; *oh my god I'm so sorry, we should exchange information for insurance,* and then a comment on his boots, or hair, or face, and getting to watch the flush creep up his oh-so-pale neck confirming that yes, he is indeed batting for the same team, and then a text a few days later, *hey, how are you doing? So sorry about the car, can I give you a ride to pick it up after repairs?* And then the ride turns into coffee, and the coffee turns into lunch, and the lunch turns into love, and there you have it folks: my future husband.

Except, it didn't go down like that, because my dumb ass forgot . . .

"Joan's Stone on Loan?" The handsome stranger reads the side of my car while holding his bleeding nose—unfortunately broken by his airbag. Which shouldn't have deployed from a mere love-tap . . . if that love-tap hadn't been backed by 1,200 pounds of premium Calacatta marble.

"Yeah." I scratch the back of my neck awkwardly, taking in the crooked logo sprawled across the side of my Subaru Crosstrek—crooked because the rear tires decided to burst with the recoil impact of the aforementioned 1,200 pounds of premium Calacatta marble currently occupying my bungee-closed trunk. "It's, uh, my business."

"You're Joan?" The stranger has to look down his pinched nose at me to ask, trying to staunch the bleeding.

"No, I'm, uh, Steven. Sorry about . . ." I gesture vaguely in the direction of his ruined Honda Civic.

"So, who's Joan? And why is there a statue of Bob Ross in your trunk? And—is that Bill Nye?"

It *was* Bill Nye, before the force of my imbecilic impact chipped off most of his nose and left ear. Insurance is *so* not gonna cover this.

"Joan is, um, Joan Didion. My pet pigeon. Dunno, just seemed fitting naming the business after her. We do statue rentals."

In my head, this would be something I revealed over our car-crash-coffee—*Yeah, I'm an entrepreneur, current gig is in government contracts, no biggie. Next will be private sector.* The middle of a crowded intersection, Subaru hood billowing smoke, assholes honking in a car exhaust cacophony is *not* the setup I'm looking for.

"Statue rentals?" Mr. Ex-Future-Husband asks.

"Yeah, when cities get called out for their old racist statues in parks and courthouses and stuff—you know, Robert E. Lee, Christopher Columbus, et cetera—they commission new ones with more socially conscious public figures. But in the meantime, they can't just leave the old problematic one up. Enter Joan's Stone on Loan. We offer a variety of inoffensive public figures to serve as interim replacements until the final statue arrives."

"But . . . Bob Ross? Bill Nye?"

"We've found that the socially conscious white man is a very popular option. We like to consider it a baby step toward having, say, a woman, or a person of color."

Mr. Ex-Future-Husband laughs, then winces and clutches his nose. "OK, that's good." He laughs again, winces again, and it's only natural for me to want to help, right?

"Here, lean forward." I put a hand on his back to guide him—sharp shoulder, warm skin, soft shirt, *big yes*. "Better to let it bleed. I'm really sorry . . ."

"Owen," he says, not shrugging my hand off (!!!). "And don't be sorry. It's my ex's car. It'll be his headache to deal with."

Euphoria—birds singing, harps playing, rainbows shining, Owen's big brown (and apparently single) eyes eating me up.

"Still, the whole . . ." I gesture vaguely at his face. "Can I take you to the doctor, maybe? Once the tow truck is here, I mean."

"Don't you have your own problems to deal with?" Owen eyes the burst tires of my crumple-nosed Subaru.

"I have problems, but I also have priorities." I shrug. "You strike me as a priority."

Owen cocks a brow—winces again too, but I ignore it, because holy cow is he cute with the eyebrow, single-cocked, like he's practiced.

"Are you coming on to me?" he asks.

"Nothing ventured, nothing gained?" I offer.

Something ventured, statue cracked, nose broken, congestion caused in both sinus and traffic form.

Owen laughs, but then the symphony comes crashing to a halt with his next question: "Is that why you decided to hit me in the first place?"

Time stops. Horns honk. Hearts break. Or at least, mine does. It's suddenly very, very hot, more than the heat radiating off summer-warm asphalt.

But then I look, and there's Owen, fucking *Owen*, brown eyes downright *twinkling* at my discomfort.

"Would you say yes if it was?" I ask carefully.

Owen considers. "If it's the last crazy thing you do, maybe. Because I just broke up with a load of crazy, and now I wrecked his car, and I'm potentially agreeing to a date with a guy who runs a socially conscious statue rental business out of the back of his Subaru and thought the proper meet-cute was a car crash, so . . ."

"In my defense, there was no other way to get your number," I counter.

"You could always pull a *La La Land* in literal stopped traffic and, ya know, just get out of your car and ask."

"You'd think I was a crazy person!"

Owen gives me a look. *The* look.

Game over.

"Wanna skip the hospital and just marry me?" I ask.

Owen laughs again, a rivulet of red running down his pale paisley shirt. "How about you buy me dinner first?"

"OK; hospital, dinner, *then* holy matrimony."

"Deal."

An Alpine Idol

Eva Kappel

How, you ask, did our little town of Alpegg, Upper Bavaria, come to celebrate the internationally famous annual Feast of the Blessed Heidi, patron of flower children and fashion victims? Well, it all happened because that stupid cow just wouldn't follow a simple instruction. Always with the head in the clouds, always her own ideas about what's best for her. Oh, I love her for it: the spirit, the sense of adventure. But *kruzifix!*, she really tests my patience sometimes.

On that fateful September day, I'd had two years to get to know her and her inclinations inside out, so I should have been vigilant, should have watched her every step. But the drive was halfway down the mountain when I noticed that I hadn't seen her since Father and I had reached the crossroads at Chamois Point and had joined our cows to the larger herd behind Farmer Zappl. But she'd been right beside me moments before we set out from our summer pastures, and she *never* left my side when I came up to see to the herd! We had bonded over several manic escapades. She enjoyed being yelled at by me while stuck in a pool of mud with pieces of the fence she'd torn down still stuck on her horns. And she just loved being called every insult under the sun while caught in a patch of brambles, being eaten alive by horseflies. She wouldn't just wander off and . . . and . . . would she?

Oh, crap!

There were no onlookers yet, this far from town and from the booze stalls, so I was able to leave my position for a moment. I slipped to the side of the road and did a quick sideways jog up and down our section. It gained me a disapproving raised eyebrow from my father, who was heading our herd.

"Something the matter, Chris?"

"No, no, everything's fab. Just checking on the ladies."

But I didn't see Heidi—and I would have known her anywhere! I ran back up the path to Sepp, who was bringing in his own small herd at the rear of the drive, and described the flower bouquet on her ceremonial headdress to him.

"Heidi? I'm sure she's somewhere."

Yeah, that was what I was worried about.

"I'm positive I would have noticed if she had wandered off into the trees, Chris."

He did have a good view of our herd from up here. Sepp had joined the drive late, at Poachers' Oak crossroads, so she must have strayed off before that. Which left a whole lot of mountain range to get lost in. She could be anywhere.

"Well, I'd better get searchin'! Thanks, Sepp!"

There was no time to lose if I was to have any chance at all of catching her this side of the Austrian border and shooing her down the mountain before the whole parade was over. I figured I had about 25 minutes, 30 max. I allowed myself one appreciative look back at Sepp; his new lederhosen flattered his calves so nicely. But then I was off.

As I trekked back up the mountain, I couldn't keep the occasional skip out of my step. It was a glorious autumn afternoon. I was glad that, for the sake of fabulousness, I had put on only the skimpiest of shirts under the bib of my extra-short pair of lederhosen. The sun had risen to the festive occasion and was giving it his all. Everything was bathed in a warm glow: the hay bales, the autumn crocuses, the first yellow leaves in the foliage; butterflies were dancing in the air all around me and the hills were alive with the sound of crickets. What a day to be gallivanting across the alms!

☘

An hour and a half later, I wasn't skipping anymore. The sun had sunk low, and night was falling early in the eastern forest, where I had descended after a sweep of the alms had yielded no results.

I had searched high and low, looked behind every stack of logs and every boulder, under every bush and every waterfall, into every cabin and every hunter's perch. Until at last, down among the oaks and briars, the faint sound of a cowbell had drawn me to the edge of the infernal abyss that is Flintsklamm: a 400-meter-long dry canyon that marks the eastern border of the town's territory. At its steepest, it had been carved some 30 meters deep into the rock by a stream that used to run out of the mountains. It's a nasty, spooky place, always in deep shadow. The bottom is covered with brambles and fallen tree branches. There is no bridge, no scenic footpath. Nobody ever goes there except the spiders and the weasels. In other words, it's the perfect spot to get lost in if you enjoy being troublesome.

And sure enough, there on an outcrop a couple of meters off the ground, I spied my tan-pelted target. She must have entered the canyon from the north, where the sheer cliff walls were petering out into gentle, grassy slopes. She had stomped up a harmless-looking ledge until the terrain suddenly got too steep and she was stranded. There was no way she could have climbed down the treacherous, moss-covered cliff from above. She would have fallen and broken every bone in her body. Or she would have gotten stuck on the second ledge from the top, starfished against the cliff wall, paralyzed with fear and full of regret about her own rashness and stupidity, not to mention her fashion choices, cursing her vanity while her scratched knees were burning and the mosquitoes were having a banquet on all that exposed skin.

Yes. Of course I had tried to climb down. I wanted to get to her as quickly as possible, see. She is my girl! I couldn't just let her die alone.

It quickly got chilly in the deepening shadows of the gorge. The cold was seeping from the clammy rock into my bones. Somewhere entirely too close by, a marten screeched and an owl hooted in answer. My teeth began to chatter.

Oh, how I wished I'd been sensible about my clothes, if nothing else! There was no audience here anyway. There was nobody. Nobody! Nobody knew where I was, nobody would come rescue me. Years—nay!, *decades*—into the future, some curious explorer would venture into the gorge and find what remained of me and Heidi huddled against the cliff, our bare skeletons locked in a last desperate embrace.

I started to sob.

"There you are!"

I didn't believe my ears at first. Half convinced I had reached the hallucinatory stage of extreme exposure, I peeked up without much expectation. Imagine my surprise when a human face looked back down at me over the rim of the cliff, and when that face turned out to belong to Raphael, of all people. *The* Raphael. The new boy in town. He had moved to Alpegg a year before from the big city, Traunstein, with a bright and bumbly Bernese mountain dog and the Tyrolean-skiing-instructor kind of good looks. On day two, he had joined our local mountain rescue team. On day three, everybody was in love him, or so I assume. Because why wouldn't you be? How *couldn't* you be?!

And now he was here, looking for me?

"Sepp raised the alarm when the cows were all in the stables and you didn't show up at the beer booth. I'm not on call this week, so I only heard about it when the search team was already leaving. But given your knack for getting stuck in high places, I figured we would need every man. So I got my kit and set out on my own."

Well, that sure revived my spirits. The audacity!

"Once! I got stuck on the stork nesting platform on the town hall once!"

"And what about when you climbed the May pole and were too scared to get down on your own?"

"That was just because I was drunk!"

"And what about during the Krampus run, when—"

"Okay! Fine! I get it: I'm an idiot."

"It's just, that's a lot of one times that I've had to pull your ass out of a pickle for one year, Chrissy."

But he sounded fake exasperated. There was smile in his voice. I mumbled something about him enjoying pulling on my ass.

"What was that?"

"Nothing. Anyway, how did you know to look for me here? This is kind of extreme even for me."

"Yeah, no joke. I remembered you once told me that Heidi likes clover more than she likes her own life, so thought I'd go where the clover is."

I turned my head gingerly and peeked down. Sure enough, every patch of grass on the wall that the sun still touched was covered in puffy pink-and-white flowers. So that was where the dumb cow had been headed! Apparently Raphael knew my own beasts better than I did myself. When had I even told him about this? Probably when I'd introduced Heidi to him the day we drove the herd up to the alms four months ago. Impressive memory. He seemed to really care about her.

"So, Mr. Messner, can I have your attention here? We'll get you to the ground in no time. It's only a few meters, but I want you secured to a rope nonetheless. I've just drilled an anchor into the rock up here. Now I'm going to come down to you and we're going to rappel to the bottom together."

"But what about Heidi?"

Raphael stepped backwards into the air. I almost let go of the rock to cover my eyes with my hands. But he was fine, just calmly walking down the vertical wall into the abyss like it was nothing. I guess to him, it was.

"We'll need a cattle harness for Heidi. I've radioed it in; they're requesting a helicopter as we speak."

"And you think she'll stay where she is and wait patiently until her flight is called while there is an all-you-can-eat buffet of wild clover right in front of her bloody nose?!"

Hysteria crept into my voice. Heidi was already getting restless again on her own perch, pawing the moss with her forehooves. I had to get to her, to calm her with my presence!

"Hey, Chrissy, what are you doing!? I told you to stay put! Can you please just do what I tell you for once in your life?"

I had made about two handbreadths' worth of way by the time Raphael came level with me, so he was able to just grab me and pull me back to the middle of the ledge. He froze me in place with a pointed look of fond exasperation and busied himself with the mountain of gear he'd brought in his backpack. Skittish though I was, he had me coaxed into a climbing harness in no time. He'd be great with the cows.

"There. I've secured you to the rope as well as to my own harness. Come on, I've got you, you may let go of the rock now."

He pulled me into his lap, which I guess was standard idiot rescue procedure.

"Remember, you can't fall anymore, no matter how hard you try."

I nodded, but held on extra tight anyway. Just to be safe. I did feel a bit vulnerable now that it was brought home to me how ill-prepared I'd been for this impromptu solo expedition. I felt awfully naked clinging against his full mountaineering get-up with only my flimsy four-inch shorts and linen shirt. Well, it wasn't wholly awful. It wasn't too bad, really. In fact . . . but I digress.

So did Heidi. Typical! I'd been distracted for two seconds, and there she went, unleashing her inner ibex, trying to get to me. Or to get to Raphael perhaps, drawn by the seductive sweet-talk of flowers and bondage games.

I shouted at her to stay put and wait, but that only seemed to egg her on. She pounded the knots of moss and ivy on the rocks in front of her, snorting impatiently when she couldn't seem to find a proper foothold. Never one to give up on her dreams, she kept on pawing and pulling again and again, until suddenly there came an almighty *CRACK* from the wall above her.

All three of us froze. There was a delay of perhaps 2.5 seconds in which we all held our breath, and then the whole heavy curtain of vines and soil and moss and clover and loose rocks that covered the strip of cliff wall between us and her, came loose and was pulled down. Triggered by the sudden motion, a huge boulder detached from the wall and crashed down in what seemed like slow motion amid all the rest of the detritus.

"Heidi, noooooooooo!" I tried to reach for her as she fell, but Raphael grabbed me by my bibs and pulled me tight against him so that I wouldn't have to watch. I buried my face in the crook of his neck and concentrated on the gentle heartbeat there until the racket had died down and the last straggling pebbles had click-clacked down. Only then did I dare to let go and turn around to face the inevitable carnage. What a sight was waiting for me!

Heidi was just fine. She had somehow surfed the landslide to the bottom of the gorge and was standing there on top of the pile of rubble and shrubbery, looking confused but safe and sound. Where the boulder had broken away from the cliff, it had uncovered a cave the size of a small roadside chapel. Raphael brought us down another couple of meters until we were level with it.

It was in fact a rock chapel. It had probably started out as a natural hole in the rock wall, but had been widened and smoothed out by human hands. At its back wall, a stone altar had been carved out of the living rock. It was covered in cloths of rare and sumptuous fabrics as well as an abundance of cups and plates and other devotional objects, all made from gold and precious stones and bronze and pearls. Everything was arranged around one spectacular centerpiece: a marmot-sized golden effigy of a saintly looking woman draped in shining garments. Above her on the wall was a partially effaced Latin inscription calling her "our blessed." I swear, for the first few moments after it was uncovered, a golden glow emanated from the cave, as well as the faint singing sound of a choir of angels.

Dangling beside me, and staring just as raptly, Raphael took my hand and clasped it tight.

Below, we could hear the first excited shouts of the search-and-rescue team from the other side of the shrubbery, and Heidi mooed a greeting in return.

☘

As it turned out, all the trinkets on the altar weren't really precious metals and jewels, but rather brass, earthenware, and glass. And the effigy wasn't made of gold, but painted wood. But it was centuries and centuries old and, the experts assured us, of the finest craftsmanship and the best state of preservation they had ever seen outside of the Bavarian National Museum. They are going to be a big attraction at our regional collection.

We inquired at the bishop's office, but there was nothing in the registers about a local *beata* from around here. Nor was there any record of a rock chapel. The townsfolk had probably kept it out of the maps for fear of looters. So, we decided to name it after the finder: The Cave of the Blessed Heidi.

The finds from the cave would have fetched a nice sum on the antiques market, the specialists said, and we (Heidi and I) and the community were owed that same amount from the government. The mayor used the town's share to have a wooden staircase built for pilgrimages up to the chapel, and I used mine to buy free beer for everyone on the anniversary of the discovery, the day we took the brand-new replica that Toni the carpenter had made of the Blessed Heidi's effigy up to her cave. The whole town turned out for the procession. We decided to do this every year from then on, the Sunday after the drive. We've done it twice now, so it's a tradition. With two parades and two street fairs in a row, Heidi Week is already becoming a tourist magnet. It's just like the Oktoberfest, only better: much more authentic.

Okay, I didn't use up my whole share for the party, I admit. I kept back a small(ish) chunk and used most of it to have a new bridle custom-made for Heidi. My Heidi that is, who is now the pride of the cattle drive, with her rose-gilded bell and five hundred Swarovski crystals glittering on her headband. The others have given me the side-eye about it, and when my father saw it, he got this new vein bulging on his forehead, but what can I say? She deserves it.

The rest of the money I used to buy a luxury dog bed for Wilma, Raphael's Bernese. She's a pet dog, not a farm dog, and we can't ask her to sleep on the bare floor every time we spend the night at my place. And now that all my cows are in the stable, we can finally get some peace and quiet, while the Blessed Heidi keeps watch and smiles over us as I lay out my outfit for the next day.

Report on Tennyson's Ulysses Attempting a Second Voyage

Martin Settle

Ulysses and his crew
never made it out of the harbor
they had to yield

three men with canes
fell overboard
you could hear the sirens
from rescue boats
at the scene

strive as they may
arthritic hands could not
hold the oars
and they were constantly leaving
their assigned places
to pee off the galley
adding a yellow tinge
to the wine-dark-seas

seeking to hoist the sail
resulted in two men not
being able to let go of the rope
they dangled moaning as the wind
caught the sail at an angle
listing the ship
Ulysses tied himself to the mast
to keep from sliding off

on shore Penelope and other wives
waited with packed lunches
as the hungry men's delusional display
of masculinity came to a conclusion
the journey to the Happy Isles
would have to be postponed
until the crew could find
new energy
after their midday naps

How to Become a Curmudgeon in 17 Easy Steps (And Still Get Invited to Dinner)

Brad G. Philbrick

I didn't set out to become a curmudgeon. No one does. You don't wake up one spring morning, stretch like a cat, and declare, "Today I shall object to air fresheners and invent a scorched-earth policy for iced coffee." It happens gradually, like the way dandelions colonize a lawn—one yellow uprising at a time—until one day your neighbor compliments your "wildflower meadow" and you respond with a 30-minute lecture about creeping Charlie while holding a trowel like a gavel.

If there's a patron saint of curmudgeonhood, it's Mr. Wilson from Dennis the Menace—baffled by everyone, allergic to nonsense, and two eye rolls away from sainthood or cardiac arrest. My father auditioned for the role daily. "This would be a great world if it weren't for the people in it," he used to say, like a blessing before dinner. He wasn't angry, exactly. He was . . . committed. Committed to standards, to common sense, to the belief that bumper stickers should be regulated and that anyone who says "Let's circle back" owes him five dollars.

For years, I resisted the family legacy. I was agreeable, generous, the sort of person who apologized to furniture when I bumped into it. But something in our modern age—perhaps the subscription-based toothbrushes, maybe the rise of QR-code menus that go dark precisely when your hunger peaks—nudged me toward the ancestral profession. The straw that broke the camel's lumbar support pillow was a self-checkout screen that accused me, with the moral fervor of a Puritan minister, of "unexpected item in the bagging area." I was buying bananas. Bananas are never unexpected. Bananas are the most expected fruit.

So yes, I have crossed over. The following is a field guide to becoming a curmudgeon with grace—a Mr. Wilson with better cholesterol, a skeptic who still tips 25% and returns his shopping cart to the corral. Follow these steps, and you too can cultivate high standards without losing your invitation to dinner.

Step 1: Develop a Principled Relationship with Lines

A true curmudgeon respects the line. We stand at respectful distances. We do not skip, we do not hover, and we do not perform the interpretive dance known as "Is this a line?" in front of bakery cases. My conversion occurred at the Indianapolis DMV, where a man cut in front of me carrying a novelty license plate that read "2FAST4U." I tapped him gently.

"Sir, the end of the line is back there."

He smiled, a wolf greeting a sheep. "I'm just asking a quick question."

"Splendid," I said. "Perhaps pose it at the back of the line. We're all scholars of the same curriculum."

The line applauded. I earned my first Curmudgeon Merit Badge: Civic Order, Basic Level.

Step 2: Honor Tools, Not Gadgets

Curmudgeons cherish the functional. We do not need a Bluetooth-enabled pepper grinder with 17 grind settings and a companion app that will, inevitably, ask for a software update mid-supper. We need a pepper grinder that grinds. Once, a gentleman told me his refrigerator had a touchscreen. "It shows the news!" he said. I asked if it kept his milk cold any better. He looked pained, like I'd asked his couch to solve math.

Step 3: Learn the Sacred Phrase "No, Thank You"

Curmudgeonhood is not fueled by shouting; it is aerated by "No, thank you."

"Would you like to try our new pumpkin-sriracha macchiato?"

No, thank you.

"Can I interest you in a store credit card with 37% APR?"

No, thank you.

"Do you want to join our rewards program? It's free—you need to give us your email, phone number, birthdate, mother's maiden name, and a list of your childhood regrets."

I deploy "No, thank you" with serene finality, the way a monk rings a bell.

Step 4: Compose a Personal Manifesto About Packaging

There is an inverse relationship between a product's utility and how hard it is to open. I once bought a pair of scissors that required a second pair of scissors to free them from the blister pack. This is not packaging; it's an escape room. Writing your manifesto—short, punchy, laminated—helps. Mine reads, "If I need protective gear to access it, I don't deserve it."

Step 5: Maintain Benevolent Skepticism of Slogans

Suppose a cereal box says, "Now with Ancient Grains," I ask which epoch. Sumerian? If a bottle promises "Farmhouse-Style," I ask whether someone named Earl or Ole was involved. Words should mean things. I am not opposed to marketing; I have even dabbled in it. But every curmudgeon keeps a little internal librarian who stamps your forehead when you misuse "artisanal."

Scott the Connoisseur of Mispronunciations

Every curmudgeon needs a foil, and mine is my old friend Scott. He considered himself an authority on food, wine, and all things sophisticated. Unfortunately, the one subject he never mastered was pronunciation.

At a Greek restaurant, the server told us about the *gyro* platter, pronouncing it correctly: "year-ro." I thought it sounded great, so I ordered one. Scott, not to be outdone, leaned forward and announced, "I'll have a *Ji-ro* sandwich."

The server gently corrected him. "That's *year-ro*, sir."

Scott bristled. "Geez, Brad, you'd think they would know how to pronounce their own food around here!"

Another time, over dinner, I ordered a glass of Merlot. I pronounced it "mer-loh." Scott corrected me: "It's *mer-lot*, Brad." Then he added, "And I'll have a glass of *Pi-not noyer*."

I tried to help. "Actually, it's pronounced 'pee-no nowar.'"

Scott waved me off. "No, no. I know what I'm talking about."

And that was that: Scott, champion of "Ji-ro" and "Mer-lot," lone defender of "Pi-not noyer." My dad's line echoed in my ears: *Some people should keep their mouths shut and let us think they're stupid instead of opening it and removing all doubt.*

Step 6: Know Your Origin Myth—and Pass It Down

Every curmudgeon has a tale that hardened the cartilage of their standards. Mine happened during my pharmacy days, when a gentleman marched up to the counter and insisted his suppositories "weren't doing a darn thing." We investigated. Reader, he had not removed the foil. He had, in medical parlance, attempted to launch a wrapped submarine. I discovered two things that day: (1) Assumptions are dangerous, and (2) sometimes the simplest instruction ("Remove foil") should be carved in granite.

Step 7: Adopt a Hobby That Involves Real Objects

Curmudgeons trust things we can hold. Gardening, woodworking, bread-baking, stamp collecting—these are the sanctuaries where we practice patience without Wi-Fi. I keep a small workbench. Nothing fancy. When the world demands I scan a QR code to read a napkin's nutritional facts, I retreat to the bench and sand a board until it obeys.

Step 8: Create a Taxonomy of Modern Irritants

This is not a list for stew and complaint. It's a field guide for managing your blood pressure. Mine has three categories:

- Harmless Nuisances: Leaf blowers at 7 a.m., people who clap when the plane lands, and any clothing item described as "athleisure formal." Solution: audible sigh, benevolent head shake.
- Manageable Offenses: Loud phone calls in small restaurants, mispronouncing *espresso* as *expresso*, or the use of "literally" to mean "figuratively." Solution: gentle correction if invited; otherwise, move your chair and silently award demerits.
- Crimes Against Civilization: Blocking the grocery aisle with an abandoned cart while composing a novel on your phone, replacing real chairs with stools that wobble, corporate emails opening with "Hey team!" before firing you. Solution: Speak up, write a polite note, and keep receipts.

Step 9: Practice Hospitality Like a Roman General

We love people—we prefer they behave themselves. The secret is to host well. Serve an Old Fashioned properly (no fluorescent cherries, please). Offer a chair with lumbar support. Feed guests until they glow. Then—key point—tell them where to put their phones. A small basket labeled "Sanctuary for Pocket Computers" suffices. My dinner parties are cheerful, screen-free, and last exactly two hours and forty-five minutes. At 8:55 p.m., I say, "This has been perfect," and hand out their coats to the people. They call me the Swiss Train of hosts.

Step 10: Master the Art of the Friendly Protest

Sometimes the world needs a note. Once, at a café where the music sounded like an argument between a blender and a foghorn, I asked if it might be turned down. "We like to keep the vibe up," said the barista.

I wrote a note on a napkin:

Dear Management,

Your coffee is excellent. Your staff is kind. Your music discourages communion with the croissant. Please consider minor decibels.

With gratitude, A Paying Fan.

They turned it down by, conservatively, two molecules. Did I change the world? No. But the croissant stopped screaming.

Step 11: Be Very Funny (Especially About Yourself)

Humor is the WD-40 of standards. Without it, you squeak and seize. My friends tolerate my little crusades because I mock myself first. "Brad," they say, "do you want a bite of my pumpkin-sriracha macchiato donut?" "No, thank you," I reply. "But I applaud the inventive fusion of autumn and heartburn." Then I eat half the donut.

Thanksgiving with Dad and Aunt Janette

Curmudgeonhood runs in the family, and one Thanksgiving dinner with the extended family, Dad showcased his talent with fortitude, annoyance in his voice, and was uncomfortably forthright.

There we were—my grandmother, aunts and uncles, cousins, Mom, Dad, and my brothers, Neal and Dean. Dad carved the turkey; the mashed potatoes were hot and steaming. Mom's sterling silver tableware clinked against her China dinnerware, and Dad sat with his family and his in-laws, quiet and still, waiting for the chance to strike like a cat or better yet, more like a snake. Dad listened to hear what was wrong, or someone was inevitably making the mistake of talking too much. This particular year, Aunt Janette took the bait. She was not, as my dad liked to say, "the brightest penny in the jar." But that never stopped her from speaking with confidence.

She launched into a lecture about the North Dakota Air National Guard jets. Her facts, unfortunately, bore little resemblance to reality. My dad, who had actually worked as a mechanic on those very jets, stiffened in his chair.

Finally, unable to restrain himself, he dropped his fork like a gavel. "Janette, you oughta know horse shit—you've been on the road!"

The room froze. My aunt blinked. Before she could recover, Dad followed up with his second classic: "Better to keep your mouth shut and let us think you're stupid than to open it and remove all doubt."

Thanksgiving shifted instantly from Norman Rockwell to courtroom drama. Dad leaned back, satisfied he had restored order to the universe, while the rest of us silently vowed to stick to safer topics, like weather and pie.

Step 12: Choose Hope

The curmudgeon is not a pessimist. We are conservationists of the human. If we grumble, it's because we've seen better, or at least we've imagined it. Hope keeps our standards from curdling into contempt. Hope is why we thank the cashier, return the cart, and leave the grocery store humming, even after a fresh skirmish with the self-checkout machine.

Step 13: Protect the Pronunciation

Curmudgeons care about words. A menu should be legible. A label should be accurate. And wine should not be ordered as "Mer-lot." See Scott, above.

Step 14: Curmudgeonhood Is Inherited at the Dinner Table

You don't choose this life; it chooses you. Or, in my case, it was served with stuffing and cranberry sauce. (See Dad and Aunt Janette.)

Step 15: January Is the Curmudgeon's Super Bowl

For most people, January 1st means resolutions and signing up for gym memberships. For pharmacists, it means the annual co-pay apocalypse.

Employers send glossy packets, hold meetings, and even provide hotlines. Yet, come January 2nd, patients arrive shocked that their $10 co-pay has become $25, or that their favorite drug has been replaced by something that sounds like Swedish furniture.

"Twenty-five dollars?!" a man once shouted at me, as though I had personally doubled the price.

"Yes, sir, but your insurance changed."

"Well, no one told me!"

Of course, someone told him. But in that moment, I was the villain. The gatekeeper. The pharmacist who, apparently, was making a fortune one co-pay at a time.

Pharmacists dread January more than anyone. We stock up on patience like aspirin. We can recite the script in our sleep: *Yes, it's different now . . . No, I can't change it back . . . Yes, I'm sure.*

If you want to see true curmudgeon champions, visit a pharmacy counter on January 2nd.

Step 16: Wage War on Wobbly Furniture

My wife and I inherited what was promised to be a beautiful dining table and antique chair from her grandmother's estate. I paid a trucking company a thousand dollars to deliver a marred table that wobbled like a carnival ride. The leaves were designed to extend the surface; instead, they collapsed with enthusiasm.

The antique rocking chair wasn't much better. Narrow, delicate, it made me wonder if people in the 1700s were smaller or simply enjoyed balancing on broom handles. Sitting in it required the precision of a tightrope walker.

Furniture should be solid. Furniture should be honest. Furniture should not require you to eat soup with one hand while steadying the table with the other.

Step 17: The Curmudgeon Abroad (Sort Of)

I've never been abroad—unless you count Canada. Which I do, because they sell milk in bags. That's foreign enough for me.

Still, I know that traveling anywhere is fertile ground for curmudgeonhood. Airports are boot camp: lines, crackling announcements, and boarding groups that seem to include everyone but you. Hotels are worse: keycards that demagnetize at the sight of your wallet, curtains that never fully close, bathroom lighting that could guide aircraft.

Crossing into Canada, I expected glamour. What I got was a friendlier Minnesota. Metric signs. Colorful money. Apologies for every purchase. And milk in bags. "Why," I asked, "do they sell milk in bags? Who asked for this?"

No one asked me. That's travel in a nutshell. Others snap photos. Curmudgeons take notes—for discussion later.

Closing Reflections

If you're worried curmudgeonhood will make you an island, rest easy. People love a curator. Once your friends realize you are devoted to comfort, clarity, and comedy, they'll seek you out. They'll ask your opinion on socks and butter. They'll text you cursed packaging and say, "Thought of you!" This is a community.

Of course, some will misunderstand. "Why are you so negative?" they'll ask after you gently point out that pancakes don't require foam. You can tell them your origin story (the foil submarine) or smile and say, "I'm positive. I'm positive we can do better."

Mr. Wilson never hated Dennis. He hated chaos. He loved his garden. He loved his routines. He loved the possibility that, with a bit of order and humor, the world could sing on key. The trick is to remember that Dennis—the human jungle in short pants—is also us. We were all boys once. Maybe we still are.

So yes: I am a curmudgeon now. I read menus printed on paper. I decline loyalty programs unless they offer points toward silence. I correct “expresso” in pencil, whispering “shh” like a librarian. And I host dinners that end precisely when they should, with a toast to everything that went right.

Because much does, a lot does—more than we notice.

Case in point: Last week, the self-checkout recognized my bananas without a sermon. A miracle? Maybe. Or maybe someone, somewhere, received a note on a napkin and said, “He’s not wrong.” That’s the curmudgeon’s quiet victory—not winning the war, but making minor, humane edits to the day.

On the walk home, I passed a lemonade stand. The sign read “Lemonade – 25 cents – Exact change please.” The cups were arranged in a precise little pyramid. The kids wore serious faces, like surgeons.

“Do you take cards?” I asked. They laughed as if I’d told the joke of the century. I gave them a dollar and waved away the change. “Put it toward your packaging,” I said. “Make sure people can open it.”

They nodded solemnly. “We will, mister.”

There’s hope for the world yet. And if you need a place to sit and consider it, I have a chair that I’ve personally tested. It does not wobble. The arms are just right. You may rest here until exactly 8:55 p.m., when I will say, “This has been perfect,” and hand you your coat—warm from the dryer, because of course I warmed it. Standards should be comfortable.

Come again soon. Bring your bananas. We’ll make sure they’re expected.

Hell's Belles

Meredith Meyer

I can honestly say that if it weren't for Tiffany Parker, I might never have ended up being a musician in life. When I was growing up in the middle of the Oklahoma Bible Belt, there weren't too many kids my age who strayed from the norm, with the exception of Colin, the kid in our second-grade class who ate paste. There were sports kids, nerd kids, latchkey kids, and marching band kids, but many of them at their core were still church kids, in one way or another.

Myself, I had no existential spiritual quandary at age 12. I'd gone to our small church's Sunday school classes my whole life, but it wasn't a big deal. I liked to sing, and participated in our local community theater's production of *The Sound of Music*—twice. My dad worked in sales and played the saxophone in a dancehall band on the weekends. My mother, a preschool teacher, played show tunes from a giant book on our piano. She took me to piano lessons every week taught by a local church organist. There, I learned how to count my fingers up and down scales, how to play Bach's easier pieces, and how to bow politely after sweating through my Easter dress at our annual recitals. But none of that made a huge impact on my later decision to become an actual musician *for life*.

I met Tiffany Parker when I started junior high school, at a seventh grade Pep Club introduction meeting. It was an unlikely encounter, especially because I hated sports in general, and had no desire to watch any games. But my mom had been in the Pep Club when she was in school, and she still had her little plum felt hat and gold pin, which I used to put on my head while she told me stories about this fun bus trip they took, or that one. Our school colors were green and yellow gold—not the best combination ever, because the colors made our puffy uniform tops resemble some sort of squash—and yet I still really wanted to own a Pep Club uniform, so there I was.

The other girls at the meeting all seemed to know each other, but I'd gone to elementary school in a different district, and as I scanned the faces for anyone familiar, I came up blank. Tiffany and I were sitting timidly by ourselves but sort of near each other on the bleachers. She said hello to me, so I scooted over, relieved to have someone to talk to. We realized we had an English class together, and as we chatted, found we had a few other things in common. We both had mean older brothers, we both had the same Amy Grant albums on cassette, and we both wanted to be in the Pep Club, even though we didn't really like sports.

In the days after the meeting ended and our uniforms were ordered, we started eating lunch together in the cafeteria. I soon learned that our similarities sort of stopped there, because Tiffany and I came from very different upbringings. This was reinforced by our daily wardrobes. She often came to school donning Ralph Lauren floral corduroy with a giant Coach purse flung over her shoulder, striding the halls effortlessly in her Cole Haan tasseled loafers, her long blonde hair freshly (but naturally) highlighted, waving behind her as she walked. I was the shortest person in my class, and had flat, mousy brown hair that wasn't straight or wavy. I had one worn-out pair of Guess jeans, and a fear of getting hit with a dodgeball in PE class while wearing the same dirty white Keds I'd had for two years. But there we were, two new friends who met by happenstance, in one of the least cool circumstances, during one of the most ungraceful times of our human lives.

When Tiffany invited me over to her house for the first time, I was definitely intimidated. The Parkers' house wasn't very far from the small apartment complex where my grandmother had lived, except they lived a few streets over on a deep cul-de-sac, in a large house partially covered by a brick wall and ivy. When I stepped inside their living room, it smelled like oak and leather, and had a lot of English-looking things in it. It reminded me of some coasters we had with little scenes of British fox hunts. Here, the large versions of our coasters hung on dark wooden walls in gold ornate frames, each one lit with its own small lamp. A dining room display cabinet showcased polished silver, and a whole set of China dishes just for Christmas. Thick forest green carpet went sprawling through the back of the house to the bedrooms, and as Tiffany led me down its path to her room, my toes pleasantly gripped the thick carpet through my socks. I tried not to stare too much.

We sat on her puffy floral Laura Ashley comforter, the kind with matching pillow shams edged in lace. The first thing Tiffany did was show me her burgundy leather bible, with her name stamped on the front cover in real 14 karat gold. She showed me how her favorite verses were underlined and highlighted. Then she carefully closed it, looked deep into my eyes, and in a concerned voice, asked me if I was a Christian. When I nervously shrugged and told her yes, that we were Lutheran, her eyes narrowed and she said she didn't know what that meant. Feeling on the spot, I tried to recall what I'd learned from the Intro to Catechism class my parents were forcing me to take. I did my best to make the Lutheran church sound groundbreaking and exotic, as I recited to Tiffany that Martin Luther started the Protestant movement when he wrote the 95 Theses, and nailed them to the door of the Catholic church. On the list, he challenged the heads of the church with 95 things he was tired of and wanted to change. Tiffany's eyes glazed over, but she was politely silent until I finished. When she then asked if I had *actually invited Jesus into my heart*, and I told her I didn't know what *she* meant, she squeezed my hand and invited me to a "Revival" at her Baptist church.

A Revival was apparently a big deal. Every single one of the "Big Three" churches had them: the First Baptist Church, the Second Baptist

Church, and the First Nazarene Church. I wasn't sure what they were reviving (my dad said their collection plate), but every mega-church with a big youth group had a Revival Week soon after school started, and that week always started with a free pizza party.

The last couple of weeks, students had come to school wearing red and white T-shirts that looked like Coca-Cola shirts, but upon closer inspection, they read *Christ is it!* in the curlycue lettering (those shirts looked a little more realistic than their Pepsi counterparts from the Nazarene church, which read *Jesus: The Choice of a New Generation*). The kids were armed with backpacks full of lemon yellow xeroxed "tickets," that proclaimed EAT ALL THE FREE PIZZA YOU WANT and JESUS SAVES in big block letters. Every day during lunch hour, they infiltrated the cafeteria like an army of prepubescent Christian soldier ants, scattering the yellow tickets onto every table. They even hit up the math club nerds and the woodshop students—who everyone was afraid of, because they smoked weed behind Little Caesar's after school, and gave themselves tattoos with X-Acto knives and ballpoint pens during class.

The Revival kids had a dedicated goal of handing out their entire yellow stack each day, touting "Free pizza! Who wants free pizza!?" to every single one of us, and we all cluelessly raised our hands, because who *didn't* want free pizza? So when I told my parents about the Parkers' house and how nice it was, I ignored my dad's grumbling about how *it must be nice to be a doctor these days*, and asked my parents if I could go with Tiffany to the Revival. My mom gave my dad a look, and he relented, because they knew I needed to make friends, and what could possibly happen at a Baptist church youth group meeting?

When Wednesday finally came around, Tiffany and her mom pulled up in a shiny black Volvo station wagon with eager faces. I was hoping they wouldn't want to come inside our house, and I ran out to the car before they could get out. When I got in the back seat, her mom turned around from the driver's seat, smiled warmly at me, and grabbed my hand. "We're so excited to have you with us!" she gushed. I smiled and thanked her. When she let go, my hand had a faint smell of perfume that lingered from her wrist. It smelled like the Christian Dior Poison samples that I'd gotten at the mall.

As we drove to the church, Tiffany reminded her mom that I was *Lutheran*, and her mom gave the same "huh" response. I wondered if I needed to give the catechism spiel all over again, but her mom kept talking, and asked gingerly if *my parents* went to church every Sunday. I assured her that they did, mostly, and she went on to tell me what a great man their youth pastor Ron was, and how he'd worked miracles in people's lives. Fortunately we arrived at the church before she could delve into all the miracles, and I hopped out of the car with relief, absentmindedly smelling her perfume again on my hand.

Tiffany and I first went into the church's "Fellowship Hall" for the pizza portion of the night. There, on the folding tables, sat tall stacks of cartoonishly oversized square boxes, which held the promised youth bait. My mouth watered and my stomach growled, but when we got up to our place in line, I was disappointed to find out that most of the pizzas were simply plain cheese, and a little cold too. As we made our way to a table with our thin paper plates of pizza, I recognized Tim Bell, who also took piano lessons from my teacher, and had the highest IQ in our class. I waved at him, but he was busy wiping pizza grease off his glasses with a flimsy napkin, and didn't see me. Tiffany and I sat down to eat, but the noisy atmosphere was a little overwhelming, and suddenly I didn't feel so hungry anymore. It didn't matter. Ron the youth pastor soon announced it was time to go in for the "extra special service," and I tossed my half-eaten cold cheese pizza into the trash.

We were shuffled into the main sanctuary, which was twenty times the size of our tiny church. Ron waited for everyone to quiet down, which seemed to take forever, then he got very serious. He announced that we would be watching a *very special film*, one that was very timely and important. "People. We are in times of crisis right now. There are many people who are falling down in this world, losing sight of God." As he went on, I looked around to see if I might recognize anyone else from school, but the lights dimmed to darkness.

The movie screen lowered from the ceiling, and on it appeared a man in a purple paisley shirt, with a mullet and a mustache. He spoke directly into the camera at us. I glanced at Tiffany. She was transfixed. On the screen, Mullet Man put one foot up on a VCR stand, leaned on one knee, and pointed to some concert footage on a small TV. I recognized a Fleetwood Mac song playing that I liked. The footage went into slow motion to show Mick Fleetwood dancing around on stage making a funny face. Mullet Man stroked his mustache and ended his introduction with the foreboding question: "Is it *only* rock 'n' roll?" I heard shudders and *oohs* flutter through the crowd around us.

The film had a pretty slow lead-up. Mullet Man kept quoting lots of Bible verses as he frowned on montages of mosh pits and guys with neon mohawks. He denounced rock music for summoning the Devil in its most scandalous forms: drugs, sex, groupies, *and* magic. He explained that many rock stars actually worshipped a man named Aleister Crowley instead of Jesus. I didn't know who Aleister Crowley was, but I was a little doubtful that a magician could really be the enemy. But all these points that Mullet Man made were mere stepping stones, escalating to the real crux of the movie: *backmasking*.

"They're subliminal backwards messages in music that are planted there, in the tapes, on purpose. *Messages . . . from Satan*." Mullet Man landed those words like a bomb. Tiffany grabbed my arm, her eyes wide in horror like she'd seen the Devil himself. I awkwardly patted her arm and whispered, "It's okay," because I didn't know what else to do.

Over and over, the film played clips of reversed Led Zeppelin and Beatles songs, after which Mullet Man would confidently interpret the garbled tape samples for us. And after each example, an *oooooh* or a gasp would flitter through the audience. "That one," Mullet Man announced, "said *Oh, Satan, you are the one who is shining*." I had to admit, after 90 minutes in, even I started to wonder if all this was actually true. I mean, it was right there on the recording tapes, right? At this point my blood sugar was dropping, and I felt paralyzed in the pew seat, weighing whether or not the voices *were* actually the Devil coming through the mixing board.

As my stomach kept growling, I thought maybe I was also seeing things, because suddenly a picture of Whitney Houston popped up on the screen. *Whitney?* I wasn't imagining it. Even her music was under fire now from our VJ host for being a "blatant celebration of adultery." He went abruptly from taking down Whitney, to standing next to a woman in a hospital bed on a life support machine. "This person," he pointed to the blonde woman with dark circles under her eyes, "is *spiritually sick* from listening to secular music." The woman in the bed limply raised an arm attached to an IV.

At that moment, all the girls in the audience started crying, including Tiffany, and hushed whispers of *it's okay*, mixed in with *sweet Jesus* and *Lord, please save us* bounced around the room. One more clip of an Ozzy Osbourne concert and my fellow audience members would have gone into complete mass hysteria. I checked my watch. How much longer could this go on? I was starting to feel dizzy. At the close of the *two hours and fifty-two minutes*, Mullet Man presented us with the big solution to all this Satanic madness: *simply giving your heart over to Jesus*.

By the time they brought the lights up, half the congregation looked like they'd been hit by tornado debris. Girls were terrorized, their cheeks splotched red with tears as their boyfriends comforted them. Some kids just sat there looking lost, hunched and holding their heads in their hands. Even though I wasn't totally sold, I still wondered if my family was going to hell, since we had a copy of the Sgt. Pepper album on vinyl. Logically I knew that most of what I had seen was *maybe* exaggerating? But I was also 12, and this was a whole new kind of peer pressure I hadn't felt before. I didn't want to feel like I was missing out on some key element to ensure I'd go to heaven.

Ron slowly walked back to the center pulpit with a cordless microphone, giving sympathetic *mmm-hmms*, *yeps*, and *I know, I knows* to the emotionally scarred crowd of freaked-out pre-teens. He then invited anyone who didn't know Jesus to come and pray with him, so we could ask Jesus into our hearts. *There it is again*, I noted. *Must be a Baptist thing*.

A bunch of adults in khaki pants sprung up in the aisles. Some wore matching navy polo shirts, with crosses on them where the Polo logo should have been; others had on sweater vests with the same cross. They all went down to the front and stood by a row of doors off to the side, which Pastor Ron introduced as the prayer rooms. Tiffany nudged me with her elbow and looked at me through her tear-stained eyes, smiling. I was confused. I shook my head no at her. I was about to pass out, and definitely didn't need to go into a prayer room right now with a stranger in a sweater vest. She nudged me again, with a less friendly look of expectation. I shook my head again and whispered, "*What?*"

When she rolled her eyes at me and pursed her lips together like she was mad, suddenly it hit me: I wasn't invited here because Tiffany wanted to *hang out* with me. I was here because Tiffany wanted to *recruit* me. She wanted to make sure that if we were going to be friends, that I was indeed a *real Christian* in the eyes of Jesus. I knew right then and there that to Tiffany, I would never surpass being anything more than her Jesus-makeover project.

Just then, her bony elbow hit the side of my rib so sharply that I jumped and got up just to take a deep breath. I mumbled that I was going to go use the bathroom and tried to head from our aisle to the back of the church to find the ladies' room. But as I made my way to the back, a woman whose name tag said "Marjorie" appeared smiling in front of me, her arms outstretched wide like she was going to give me a hug. "Oh, I just need to find a bathroom, ma'am," I whispered. But Marjorie was forging ahead, already pushing me backwards, scooping me with her wide arms like a snowplow, guiding me backwards toward the direction of the prayer rooms. "No, I—"

"Don't resist. Jesus loves you. Be not afraid," Marjorie insisted. As I threw a desperate glance over at Tiffany and mouthed the word *bathroom?,* she just smiled approvingly, her blonde head tilted to one side, nodding quietly along with the other people in our row. When I surrendered to Marjorie's bulldozing, I caught the other kids in the pews giving me a look of sympathy, but with an undercurrent of something . . . slightly sinister? My cheeks got hot as I felt their eyes on my back, boring into me, as if instead of walking to the prayer room, I was being taken to walk the plank. Marjorie opened a prayer room door, and just when I thought I was going to scream, I passed out.

Tiffany later said she knew it was the healing work of the Lord. When I came to and felt strange hands on my forehead, and heard the adults whispering, "Praise Jesus," it took me a moment to remember where I was. Thankfully someone brought me some Sprite in a Styrofoam cup. After a small Bible got shoved into my hands with a few church pamphlets, Tiffany helped me out to her mom's car, glowing the entire way. As I got into the back seat, I'd never been more excited to go home.

"Well, girls?! How was it?" Tiffany and her mom seemed to be exchanging secret codes with their eyes.

"She did it. She asked Jesus into her heart!" Tiffany smiled and patted my arm. They cooed and cheered, and her mom looked at me funny. I must have been a sight in her eyes, like a pale street urchin who had been lost, but now was found. "Oh, *honey*, we are so happy for you. This is the beginning of a new time for you! He will never *ever* leave you."

"Yay," I mustered, giving it the best enthusiasm I could.

I almost got carsick on the ride home, but finally stumbled in through the front door, *thank Jesus*, where my parents were sitting watching the nightly news. They barely glanced at me as I came in. I went directly to the fridge, got some orange juice, and guzzled it, trying to bring myself back to life.

"Well?" my dad said, keeping his eyes on the TV. "How was it?" I didn't even know how to try, or want to try telling them about the movie. So I shrugged.

"It was okay," I said flatly. "I think . . ." I steadied myself on the back of a chair. "I think I'd like to learn how to play the guitar."

Cat People

Dar Thomas

When my gaze traveled to the birdbath that lovely Sunday morning, it came to me in a shock that what I was actually seeing was only its column—snapped off! At the precise point where it *should* have met the bowl, which, I next discovered, lay about it in three distinct pieces on the ground, like a decapitated crown. I hadn't really expected the tenuous structure to remain intact forever: the cracked—but still noble—column retrieved from a local flea market, the newly purchased, cerulean-glazed saucer perched regally—and evidently, precariously—atop. Regardless, I knew, beyond a doubt, that the next-door cats were to blame for this new disaster: this but another squall in the tempest of destruction those two feline despots had rained on me in just the last year.

Believe me, had I any foresight as to the ordeals I was to face in the surprising perennial decline of my locale—home of my 40 years as Whiteboro citizen, mother of two fine (moral and married) daughters, and proud wife of Councilman Henry Antonelli, who, I've come to appreciate, served as a subtle buffer between my sensibilities and our mutating environs (yet left me in his sleep almost three years ago—on soul-shattering Christmas eve, nonetheless!)—I may well have quitted the charms of my beloved domicile: our elegant, late nineteenth-century estate house, around which a flourish of ostentatiously modern houses with their new breed of occupants had encroached, through the years, like crab grass in a rose garden.

And I must tell you, in all my lifetime, even my years of teaching high school English, dealing with those irascible students of the genre, so enamored of themselves (as were we all at that stage of the game, of course), thinking themselves so sophisticated and erudite, so worldly, so worthy of all life's advantages and, thereby, advancing their rights and freedoms—I've *never* experienced such brass, such flagrant *disregard* for others, as I have with too many of my neighbors.

Over the years, I've come to know these people all too well: their overblown hilarity, coquettish conviviality, and contrived camaraderie, derived from their special brand of "friendship," which informed me, when I'd see them at their fences, heads bobbing like Halloween apples, they'd be talking about whichever one of them was absent from the scene.

Furthermore, I can honestly say—and it was solely for the sake of civility, not for any want of membership in their coffee clutches and backyard gossiping—I had truly outdone myself. Yet, in all of my efforts to extend grace and patience, I seemed fully unable to secure any hope of insight or conscience (theirs) or some semblance of reasonable peace (mine).

A primary example of what I was up against: to my right, her open-windowed house situated so that it blocked the better part of the rising sun, her country-"music"-blaring radio consuming most of my Saturday mornings, lived Horsewoman—a pseudonym, of course, my feeble attempt to infuse some levity into the inanity around me. Horsewoman, ranging the span of our shared border, a supposed boundary defied by her very essence, manifested in an explosion of flesh and bone thrust up from the center of her immense, undulating hips—like those of the palomino my parents gave me for my sixteenth birthday (a gnarly, spirited beast who bit at me and strove to squash me in the stall every chance she got, ironically named Gem)—Horsewoman's mass-matching bluster and brimstone-hurling temper profaning open air with the force of a rodeo-pricked bronco (No, *not* stretching the metaphor here; and neither would I paint such a repugnant picture, if she would just be . . . *civilized*!).

Years back the object of Horsewoman's ire had been her young son: puff-eyed, pale-skinned Paul. I'd always felt such a confusion of angst and pity for Paul. Such a pathetic, seemingly dimwitted boy (but smart enough, in the summer he turned four, to snap the heads from my prize dahlias)—that I couldn't bear to allot him a nickname other than just *Poor Paul.*

Then, suddenly it seemed Poor Paul was not four—or six or eight—anymore. And one day I noticed he'd effectively disappeared. My thoughts, of course, veered naturally toward his demise—Horsewoman's open-windowed threats still echoing in my head, like the ringing in your ears that lingers after the flu: "I'll kill you before I let you talk to me like that!"

Then again, I rationalized, most probably Poor Paul, having reached those parentally arduous teen years, had been spirited off—perhaps by some previous, mutual, agreement—to live with his father. "An immature, irresponsible, golf-pro wannabe" who'd absconded with "some flippy Florida model" is how I recall Viola Fintsen (aka Miss Vixen—Horsewoman's friend and the occupant of the dinky stone house down the street, upgraded the exact number of times she's entertained "gentleman friends"), described it to another neighbor, one day as we waited at the bus stop.

It amused me that those people must have thought the bun on the back of my head was some kind of valve that shut off my ears or brain—or both. I guess they thought that just because my hair was whiter than my teeth, I was some befuddled old soul dithering along, toward that final, tenuous edge of life. It was all too evident they didn't read *Health* or *Prevention*. If they had, they might have considered that I could race-walk circles around their silly strolls (yet another occasion for their schoolgirl gossip) and bike the neighborhood hills like a nanny goat on holiday. Then again, with one's nose pushed so firmly into one's own navel (Henry would say something else), it was probably difficult to notice much in the larger world.

Anyway, for those three weeks with my car in the shop, confined to that tiny bus-stop kiosk, I couldn't help but hear their stories. And those women seemed to expand (and I do mean in the literal sense) in direct proportion to their verbiage, so that, as their "theories"—and extrapolations thereof—advanced, I had to continuously inch away to escape being subsumed into their mass. Like a victim of that Blob creature (a favored horror when my Emily—David's mom—and Amanda were growing up). Of course, I'd simply feigned deafness and fixed my smile on a spot beyond those chirpies, all the while contemplating how seriously happy and humbly appreciative I would be when my Caddie (sweet, old, loyal thing of a car) would be out of the shop.

At any rate, the first few years after Poor Paul had gone were lonely years for Horsewoman, judging by the absence of any other life in her house, save that of the multifarious cavalcade of pets: a small yappy dog with oily, red eyes and trembling toenails, painted crimson to match its pitiable orbs; a large, mostly silent bulldog, who left huge, fluid, steaming deposits so close to the chain-link fence between our yards that they oozed through the loops into my peony patch; a ferret who bit Horsewoman on the flatulent pouches of her cheeks; and a parrot she attempted to balance on her shoulder the same spring she took up rollerblading on the street after dinner each evening, a debatable—but brave, I had to admit—endeavor on her part.

Then some indeterminate time later (time, I've found, flies regardless of the presence of fun), I was alerted to the recurring visitation of a new friend: a large but sheepish, fair-haired, flaccid-skinned man. It was hard to avoid noticing, as they romped around that chain-linked plot, at all times of the day and night, carrying on in such exhilarated tones as to beg attention to their mutual, newfound success with each other. As if each were, somehow, proof the other was not, as David (whose youth allows such inexperienced cruelty, which I would never permit if they were nice people) would say, a "total loser" and a "major dweeb."

In retrospect, however, that convivial noise was a blessing compared to the bombastic abasement Horsewoman began levying—was it the very day of their wedding?—at her newfound *husband*, aka Pony Bill, a nubbin of a man with that watery, white flesh, puddled like unbaked bread dough at his elbows and knees, all of which was accentuated by a generally impotent demeanor which, God help me, seemed to beg abuse.

It wasn't difficult to see why Pony Bill immediately set about contriving alliances with his rear neighbor Bill Fitzgibbon, (aka Big Mouth Bull Frog), so named for his habit of behaving in the manner of an obstreperous 13-year-old with bad skin, eternally bellowing things like "My man Bill! Givin' the wife a thrill?" and "How's it hangin'? Up and bangin'?" which I'm certain must have gone a long way in Pony Bill's mind to assure him of his manhood, to prove that he, indeed, still had his *cojones*, as Bull Frog referred to them, as he posed on the elevated platform of his new plastic-railed deck, Cro-Magnon paw clawing at his own. (*Huevos* is the word they actually want, David informed me.)

Still, as difficult as Bull Frog and Pony Bill and Horsewoman were to ignore, as arduous a task as it was to tolerate them at times, none have made my life as miserable—indeed, they seemed, as my dear Henry (God rest his soul) would say, "*hell bent* on taking me down"—as the people to my left: the Cat People (yes, I was now fully surrounded).

The Cat People: owners of the two aforementioned creatures; a somewhat newly married couple (although, unless they were at the police station filing a complaint against someone, she went by a last name other than his), who made me wonder how, on God's green earth, two so equally mean-spirited, rude, and, as David would say, "seriously uglified" people could ever have found each other. And perhaps it was simply that, I thought: the genetic curse of their mutually dour countenances and general physical (mis)demeanors had predisposed them to one another—and to the grudge they seemed to hold against the rest of the world at large. And, of course, given my unhappy proximity, against me in particular.

From the very day they moved in—another grand, old, architectural masterpiece, whose elegant guts they immediately ripped out, replacing hardwood, porcelain, and silk wallpaper (as per curb-trash evidence)—with various forms of plastic, acrylic, and all manner of unnatural modernity (big-truck deliveries announced by snarling engines and putrid fumes)—they spoke to no one. Even approached face-on, within arm's length, they would screw up their faces—his as fleshy and pallid as his pate was starched and freckle-pocked; hers with cheeks like boiled potatoes, her nose like an over-ripe zucchini, and hair that, David laughingly said, "begs a cage"—and they'd look right past you. As though you were some unlikely and wholly unwelcome apparition.

Then, three years after they moved in, along came Charlie, their only saving grace; which proved my theory that God is totally impartial—and perhaps unfairly so—in the dispensation of justice. Charlie: sweet, dimple-faced, blue-eyed, chuckling, cooing, charisma-oozing Charlie. Born to those two.

It seemed Cat Woman had lost twins the year before. I learned this from my one verifiable friend (and confidante) in the neighborhood, Rachel Avedeen, who was my singular assurance that I was not seeing things "bassackward" as Henry would say. And the only reason Rachel, who, even as a "modern" woman barely into her forties (although with her moonbeam skin, she looked barely half that) and tended to be as private as I, knew about Cat Woman's personal loss was that, one day as she was walking by the Cat People's plot on her way to my house, she became the unsuspecting recipient of Cat Woman's sudden outburst of grief. Yes, without warning, Cat Woman pounced from her stoop, trounced over to Rachel, and huffing and puffing to keep Rachel's pace, blurted out, between stolen snorts of breath, every dreadful detail of the sad saga.

Well, needless to say, when Rachel told me of this tragedy, I felt deep chagrin. I remember thinking, most particularly, as Rachel unfolded this startling information, that if I had known Cat Woman was struggling with this burden, I would surely have dismissed a great part of her rudeness, purely on that account. After all, even the worst of us deserve a little patience and grace—a little extra space—at such times.

But then—and I truly do not know why anything surprised me at that point—as it turned out, her story was all a dream. Literally. The whole damn drama. Another neighbor later told Rachel she overheard Cat Woman at church, telling the minister how she had dreamed the entire twin-death episode and had awakened in such a state of hysteria that she thought it was real. Cat Woman said she only told everyone the story, because she actually lived with the twin tragedy as her reality for over three weeks. And during this time, she was so thoroughly distraught that she shut Cat Man, who "refused to feel her pain," out of the house. She demanded he stay at the downtown Hilton and refused to answer his calls, so she could "deal with her tragedy"—among "many other issues"—and get her "head back together" without his "constant nagging."

So anyway, along comes Charlie. Now wouldn't you think the presence of that charming prince—a gift if I ever saw one (it made one seriously consider that baby-switched-in-the-hospital thing you'd see on the cover of the checkout-line tabloids; and it made one think, too, of the poor folks on the less-fortunate end of that particular mix-up, stuck with the shocking evidence of Cat People's coupling)—would have been enough for those people to forego the duo of cats? After all—and it is *not* just an old wives' tale—babies and cats do not mix. For a lot more reasons than the suffocation issue.

But no, not the Cat People. Even with darling Charlie, those evil felines maintained their reign, expanding their realm to become the malevolent marauders prowling my domain, desecrating everything in their path.

At first, when the wide swaths of dead grass, roughly circular in shape, began to show against the fresh, spring green of my front lawn—discovered from my upstairs window one morning, as I looked out fondly upon my darling dogwoods, blooming their hearts out below—I had to admit I was clueless. I laughed out loud when Rachel wryly suggested that some alien spacecraft was landing at night, using my yard as a repository for their alien detritus. And ignorant as I was at the time, regarding the habits of feline creatures, I had no alternate explanation for the "Cheerio-grass" (David's contribution) phenomenon. Nor had I any real understanding of the strange, "totally gross" masses, which looked like perverse entanglements of intestines and hair, left on my back porch door mat—once even on the hood of my sweet Caddie! ("Furballs," Rachel would soon inform me.)

In short order, my flower gardens began to falter. I discovered the first evidence of this dastardly decline one Saturday morning, as I came out on the back porch to have my first coffee. My ferns and carnations appeared to have been part of a knitting party. My daisies and cornflowers sprawled on the ground as if they'd been giant-stomped. And most heinous of all in the crimes against the little haven I've tried so diligently to maintain in the midst of this insidious plasticity, all around my yard and garden arose a horrific stench. It was undeniable (for a while I tried to persuade myself that it was a function of my overwrought imagination) and so potent that one day, as I was mowing my grass (a careful mixture of Kentucky blue and rye, I'd sown myself), the stench overwhelmed me; and as I struggled to empty the lawnmower bag, thinking that therein lay the problem, a swarm of tiny, crazed flies engulfed me, as though I myself were some huge, seamy, excremental deposit.

At just that moment, up the street came Rachel. "You've got a cat problem," she announced, sniffing the air and backing away from me and my circus of flies. "Your aliens are cats, Madeline," she said, screwing up her fine nose. “Cats with a capital *C*,” she added, and pressing those lovely, red lips of hers together, she gave me such a look of pity. As though she knew something I didn’t about such matters.

Later, when I thought about what Rachel had said, it brought back a recollection: a vacation house at the beach—Nags Head, I think it was—which had a bedroom where a cat had stayed (and sprayed). Henry tried everything to disappear that odor. But it hung in the air like a massive, obstinate cloud of flatulence, so we finally gave up and just closed the door on the room. Emily and Amanda slept on a foldout couch in the sitting room of the place for the full week.

Well, suddenly everything made sense. And now that I knew what was desecrating my property, befouling the very air I breathed, those cats—in open defiance of the Whiteboro ordinance against outdoor cats—were everywhere. During the day, they stalked my garden, leapt at my bird feeders, absconding through the hemlocks like thieves running from daylight. At night, driven by that feral energy they couldn’t escape, they groaned and howled outside my windows, hissed and shrieked at enemies in the dark, or attacked my sleeping creatures, turning my peace-giving birds, rabbits, and chipmunks into screaming meemies.

Many an anguished night, deranged with my powerlessness over this senseless injustice, I would throw myself out of bed, pull on my gardening gloves, and stalk from the house to prowl the darkness, the flashlight and the ball bat from under my bed in hand, as I searched for those miscreants, swearing to myself that I’d annihilate them—those mindless marauders—without a single moment’s thought. “I will feel no guilt,” I told Rachel. “Not one iota.”

Once I actually caught one: the lead cat, I thought, because he seemed to always show up a few minutes ahead of the other one. Milton, his name was—I knew this, because Cat Woman would call the cat, bleating out his name (although it could have been the other one that time, i.e., Socks)—as though the unwitting beast would heed her and trot home like an obedient dog. (She probably had more luck with that wimpy husband of hers, whom she called in the exact same way.) At any rate, I actually caught one that summer night, crouched like a coward in the center of a patch of shock-faced dahlias, a tiny ball of squealing fur clamped in his evil mouth. Stunned by the beacon of my flashlight, which glinted off his eyes like hot, white coals, Milton froze, whereupon I grabbed that overfed, domesticated demon by the scruff of his neck with one hand, and with the other, I wedged my fingers into the back corners of his malicious mouth, and pried with all the might of Heaven, until he let that bunny baby go. Then, with him still firmly in my clutches, I peered into the darkness, hoping to spot his evil companion who, I was sure, lurked nearby, cataloguing my every move for some later revenge.

I was, however, denied the discovery of his collaborator. So I took the furtive feline back to the Cat People's house, pushed him in through the cat flap on the bottom of their back door, and scooted their milk box up against the opening to prevent his re-emergence into the night. It was my hope, also, that when Socks came home and found himself shut out, he would carry on in the same manner he employed at my house, and give his oblivious owners a taste of the bitter medicine they were so loathe to swallow: the truth about their despotic "meow-meow, kitty boys," as I overheard Cat Woman purring to them one day in their back yard—just before I had to rush out to rescue a dove who had flown into my sunroom window and lay on my porch in a daze, drowning itself in a dirge of pitiful cooing, certain to suck in old Milton and his cohort.

It was, in fact, that very day that I admitted to myself that things had gotten out of hand. This particular epiphany occurred within a mere matter of days since I had come home from my walk to discover the gut-wrenching remnants of an obliterated robin nest, the gingery smear of newborn bird flesh mauled into the rose-chintz cushions of my wicker swing. A horrific event, which followed on the heels of the tragedy of the previous week, whereupon I was to discover the blood-smudged hollow of downy bunny fuzz at the base of my broken tree peony.

It was thus that I found myself in a state of full emotional disarray. Vigilance and alarm, I realized, had become my constant companions. I could find no peace. My Garden of Eden had become an alley of evil. And I had to admit, for the first time I could remember since Henry's death, I was total loss as to what to do about it.

Finally, on a morning three days later, as I was repotting a crock of Reiger begonias (knocked to the floor of my porch by the feline forces of the night), it suddenly dawned on me that there would be no end to this—unless I took it upon myself (as Jean-Luc Picard would say) to *make it so*.

Indeed, Captain. I would take charge, become, as the current fashion termed it, *proactive*. I would simply visit the Cat People, have a little chat with them, in a decent, civilized, reasonable manner about this wholly avoidable problem. The only rational way to approach the situation was to take responsibility. Summon the courage.

So, after much fraught debate—with myself, with my daughters, with Rachel, whose vote of confidence I failed to garner: "I *don't* think they've been de-clawed," is how she put it, winking one of her big, blue eyes at me—I made up my mind to address the problem forthrightly, and to do so, for the sake of my own dignity if for nothing else, with as much diplomacy as possible.

Hindsight being hawk sight, that tactic was perhaps my first mistake; for it seemed, as was made evident to me right off the bat, such people have little respect for anything short of a hearty whack of verbiage. "They probably think you're a wuss," David told me.

Regardless, attuned to a more altruistic—and animistic—philosophy, I made up my mind to present my case and, in the process, refrain from saying anything regarding the obvious fact that their creatures could only be wholly unhappy, that they were, in essence, taking out their hostility on (too accessible) me for dear, sweet Charlie's imposition on their lives—a possibility the Cat People, with their various limitations, would, perhaps, never be able to fathom.

I can still see it, that inane scene in which I placed myself, even after Rachel, to her credit, tried desperately to spare me: "You inhabit the same planet," she said, finally, and tilted her sage head at me, as though this were something I must surely, myself, recognize. "But you live in *totally* different worlds."

"There's always the chance they'll see the light," I told her. "Someone's got to tweak their worldview. Right? After all, Evil prevails when good *wo*men do nothing," I added with conviction and had the fleeting thought that, after a lifetime of living by that tenet, I'd forgotten who'd said it.

Rachel, however, wasn't swayed. Regardless, I persisted in my illusion that I could, somehow, find justice in this. Make it all come out right somehow. After all, is not rudeness merely the defense of people made small by their insecurity? Not that calling up that bit of wisdom would make this event any easier.

"If all goes well," I told David, who was already entertaining thoughts of how we could celebrate our Saturday together—after the "conference."

Over veggie plates and watermelon, we'd been discussing "the situation," when suddenly David made the unfortunate comment roughly aligning my backyard oasis with a hunter's salt-lick setup.

That did it. I needed to make history of this. Right then and there.

"Dream queen," he said, shaking his head but giving me his fond grin and a big high-five, as I left him and our unfinished lunch, which we had been enjoying enveloped in the fabulous fragrance of my glorious ivory-silk lilac (whose voluptuous, cantaloupe-sized blooms burst open in early summer, unlike their counterparts of an earlier season).

Around to the front of my house, I bounded to the street, where in the space of seventeen strides, with my heart skipping in my throat like a kid's jump rope, I turned down the Cat People's new sidewalk—for which they'd *willingly* uprooted a charming path of fieldstone and sacrificed a story-high rhododendron and two delicate red maples. All this, I thought not without ire, for this audacious swath of concrete. A purposelessly meandering serpent of cement slithering through the acrid sea of their chemically "enhanced" lawn, only to be severed like an architectural afterthought at the elegantly domed front door. (My next thought was to give them credit for at least keeping the stately mahogany door, but then they probably hadn't had time to find a dome-shaped hunk of metal to replace it.)

From the first moment, as I arrived on their stoop, attempting to dislodge something gritty from the soles of my sandals (kitty litter, I imagined), scrubbing it off (as if they might actually invite me in) on their doormat, which, to my amazement, bore the rubberized images of two tire-sized, feline faces (a designer piece? I wondered, awed at the possibility), each emblematic cathead bearing the outline of a crown, nonetheless—I knew I was doomed.

Sun hat in hand like some supplicant, I winced against the harsh brilliance of that surprisingly simmering day, and strove to quell the roil of my jumpy tummy, as it revolted against the malodorous smog emanating from their screen door: a rank complicity of grilled flesh (probably the customary "burgers" enjoyed by creature eaters) and something vaguely familiar, like sour milk or diapers (or what I imagined—ugh!—the reek of kitty-soiled litter).

Having come this far, however, I knew I would regret even the thought of (cowardly) retreat. Even under these circumstances. Therefore, fingering the lucky stone in my pocket and turning a blind eye to the vulture of doubt encircling my brain, I steeled myself and began, ever so judiciously, selecting and connecting the delicate strands of words that might convey the simple solution to the situation: Follow the ordinance: keep your (frigging) cats inside.

"It's not that I have anything against the cats," I imagined myself saying, as I stood there sweating green tea and lemon. "I love *all* the creatures." And this was true. It was a shame, really, this having to choose. But when it came to the line between the defenseless birds and squirrels and bunnies (I'd like to see those pussies tackle that broad-racked buck, who cruised through my backyard every now and again), I had nowhere to take my stand but on the side of the underdogs. Especially, I felt, because my sanctuary did—as David's painful analogy brought home to me—give these small denizens a false sense of security and in essence—but only because of the presence of those cats—made them even more vulnerable.

"Survival of the fittest," my well-intended Amanda had tried to argue, long distance from San Diego. As if that case had any leg to stand on.

"Bully bunk," I told her in no uncertain terms. The cats did not need to hunt the suburbs to survive. They had lovely designer bowls from which to sup their milk and masticate their meaty morsels. My creatures had only the bounty of the earth from which they, by themselves, with no helpful hand—and with a plethora of *natural* predators added to the challenge—had to procure their livelihoods.

Yes, of course, I knew that such a stand "against" the cats would not bode well with many; as, if the adverts were any indication, it seemed those independent creatures had become quite popular. I had, however, always liked to think of myself as a woman of *principle* rather than of popularity (prom queen: been there, done that. Yawn). Furthermore, as much as I did not fancy confrontation of any sort, there were just some things one could not dance away from. I knew in my heart of hearts, I had no alternative. I had to assume my responsibility—and somehow persuade them to see theirs. Yes, I had to stand my ground. Period.

"Milton and Socks would *never* leave our yard," Cat Woman purred, dramatically, as the dastardly duo wore themselves out against her stalwart shins, pausing now and again to glare up at me with those glittering, wide-eyed orbs of deception and that sadistic smile of theirs, which I was sure, if they were capable of such cognition, they would think beguiling.

Cat Man, who'd pushed into the space next to his wife behind the screen door, stared at me with his flat eyes, making no pretense of cordiality, as he continued to nosh away at whatever he'd been eating. Finally, through his food-infested teeth (not one prone to swallowing before opening his mouth, I learned), Cat Man managed to masticate a few words.

I could have sworn he said, "What the fuck?"

God almighty, I snapped at myself in my head, *he couldn't really have said that!* and summoned the instant counter-thought that he'd probably said something like "What's up?" or "What's funny?" Although I'm sure, as comical as he looked, I would have allowed *nothing* to show on my face. Perhaps, I thought, with my brain all tied up in the orchestration of this sensitive conference, I'd just heard him wrong or confused the words. Which is easy enough for anyone to do.

A perfect example: The other day, I was on my way back from the farm market (for which, ironically, I must travel to the city), when I was stopped in a line of construction traffic to make way for a monster machine to cross the road. I couldn't help but notice the awesome immensity of the thing and its massive yellow belly of iron, on which was inscribed in large, black letters: "LIEB HERR." I laughed out loud—"love master"—and then really cracked up, as in the next second I saw my error: it was L*I*EB (work) not L*E*IB (love) master. Language can be tricky that way. Even more so in its more transient *aural* form. (Plus my hearing might be a tad off. I keep hearing bizarre things like subject pronouns being used as objects—e.g., they warned he and I); the preposition *at* affixed to the end of sentences (wondered where he was at). Just the other night, I heard Rachel Maddow, of all people, actually say the *at* thing and, even worse, presidential *libary*!)

"How you know they're our cats?" Cat Man had pushed into the screen door and demanded, now with an empty—yet fusty—mouth. Then eyes darting over me like a crazed hummingbird, he clawed his hand across the astounding protuberance of his T-shirted abdomen, exposing the gaping hole of his navel. Which looked—I tried to avert my eyes—just too much like one of those hairy, brown caterpillars you find curled up in a dark corner of the garage or under a leaf. And God help me (and forgive this rare pulse of schadenfreude), for in that moment, I allowed my myself the delightful image of Cat Man in full-body duct tape.

But now all at once, without missing a beat, Cat Man swiped his mouth on the forearm of his T-shirt and bolted back into the house. Before I could open my mouth to answer. Before I had a chance to even think about addressing the destruction of my property, my yard, and my gardens (the repair of which would soon impose on my finances to the tune of nearly seven-hundred big ones).

Cat Woman looked at me, a smug smile lifting her jowls, as though some victory had been won. "Listen, *Hon*," she began.

Okay, Cat Lady. I answered her in my head, attempting a split-second glance-away, so as not to bear witness as she pawed her underarm, then smudged her hand across her nose. To you, that would be *Attila. Comma the—*

"Next time you *think* you see our cats"—she picked at a tooth, sucked something from her finger—"you just come on over and tell us, Hon," she said with a lilting tone of finality, which I'm sure she thought was sarcasm, and shut the door in my face. "She wouldn't know wit if it kissed her on the lips," Rachel would snark later, over a shared plate of Boursin and homemade sourdough bread.

That night I sat, sadly resolute, on my porch, a bottle of Malbec, my flashlight, and pistol—the pistol my father once used to protect us kids from copperheads who got into the stables—next to me on the table. About 2 a.m., according to my Bulova the last time I'd checked, something moved in the hemlock nearest the edge of the porch. First there was just a slight twitching of the lower limbs, then a kind of nervous trembling, which moved upward through the boughs. There was no doubt in my mind: those cats were in there. Skulking toward some innocent bird's nest!

Without any real forethought as to exactly how I would manage this event—but convinced that I must not hesitate when the time came—I flashed the light, caught the evil gleam of eyes, aimed between them, and pulled that trigger. It was that quick. That simple. The pistol cracked, a sound really no more remarkable than a firecracker or a small car backfiring. A compact, I thought, pleased that it was nothing more chaotic or dramatic. A two-door Honda civic, perhaps.

The hemlocks fell still. The eyes were gone. I anticipated the second round. Milton was always the first to arrive, but Socks had to be somewhere nearby. I sat totally still, careful not to creak the wicker. My forearm and hand rested on the table, my hand wound around that slim pistol butt, index finger curled over the trigger. But nothing stirred. I lowered my hand and cradled the gun in my lap, my fingers still poised for action.

After what seemed like an eternity, nothing had happened, and I decided I should call it a night. My back ached (the small of my back, the cross of the ex-dancer), and I felt a kind of all-over heaviness. Tomorrow was another day, I reasoned—and of course, the distasteful afterthought instantly registered: I'd have to dispose of Milton or, perhaps, as irony would have it, Socks. But I forced myself to let it go and went to bed. Where, for some bizarre reason (escapism, perhaps?), I slept the first sound, uninterrupted sleep I'd known in many months.

The next day was Sunday again. *Perfect*, I thought. All the neighbors (the wives mostly) would go off to church (which always made me wonder what those churches were doing wrong) or sleep in (the husbands mostly). I would simply find Milton or Socks, whichever the case may be, dig a hole in the back of my garden behind the peonies, and cover the grave with wood chips. With one cat mysteriously disappeared—and I must tell you, at that point, I felt only the slightest tinge of guilt, for I was as desperate as those people were obstinate—perhaps the Cat People would come to their senses.

So I waited until all the churchgoers drove off—not that anyone could actually see into my backyard—just to be on the safe side. A surprise visitor was the last thing I needed to deal with, as I carried out my shameful plan to bury the neighbor's—those arrogant, crass, mean, short-sighted people who had forced me into this foul deed—pet. I still seethe when I think of how I was goaded into even considering that heinous act. A crime against my very nature. And I cringe when I recall myself, skulking out from my basement door, gloved, hatted (the one with the widest, down-turned brim, of course), shovel in one hand, trash bag in the other, feeling like some major miscreant.

Yes, there I stood, leaning on my shovel, "*scoping out* the crime scene," as David would put it, when what I *should* have been doing on this lovely Sunday morning was having coffee on my back porch with the sweet smell of hemlocks and the excited, gap-mouthed twittering of birdie babies, the arts section of the Sunday paper my only concern.

I don't know what it is about Sundays that's so special to me. I get a similar feeling on Thursdays. A *thrill* is about the only way I know to describe it. Which leads me to think (although the credit for this rationale truly goes to Rachel, the analytical one, who proposes that *story* lies within *history* for a reason) that perhaps it *is* because the Sundays—as well as a few other wedges of my childhood time pie—were virtually devoured by the seemingly insatiable appetite of my parents for such joy-defying activities as Wednesday-night prayer meetings and Sunday services (a.m. and p.m.!), the tenets of which were so faithfully pursued by those ardent adults, who misguidedly thought that to "train up a child in the way he must go" meant anchoring their progeny's boredom-bruised bottoms to the austere planks of those pitiless pews, from which they were forced to endure an eternity of hell-fire diatribes; so that, at the very first whiff of independence, those very children (yours truly at the head of the pack), against all intentions of their adult mentors, did indeed, as quickly and thoroughly as possible, "depart from it."

Rachel might be right on the mark, for I do remember, so vividly—almost painfully—how I grew to dread the approach of those torturous days. Especially once I'd learned (sleep-overs sometimes included Sundays, during which my parents surprisingly allowed me to attend my friends' churches) that the shabby events conducted by *my* church were so unlike the glamorous rituals of my friends' cathedrals, exotically steepled and glowing with exquisite rainbows of glass, while my "house of God" (my mother's term) more resembled a Velveeta-cheese box with wax-paper portals. Their minister was "Reverend" or "Father" so and so. Our "man of God" was plain, old "Preacher Bob."

To add insult to injury, I learned that my friends' parents condescendingly referred to our church as the "holy-roller chapel on the hill." Furthermore, courtesy of their religion's benevolent creed, they were *not* forbidden to smoke or drink or even—to my eternal astonishment—to "take God's name in vain." And they all watched TV on Sunday, without blinking.

I would have given anything to be able to see just one of those shows, to just once, on a Monday at school, be able to throw in my own comment on Tinker Bell or Dr. Dolittle. I just wanted to be a *normal* kid like everybody else!

I admit, fully, to the marvelous sense of relief I felt (that thrill!), once I had gone off to college and returned home only for holidays or an occasional weekend, when suddenly it seemed I had a *choice* in the matter. No longer was I awakened on Sunday mornings. In fact, as I lay there in my bed, feigning study-exhausted slumber, I had a strong sense that my parents were being purposely—and extravagantly—quiet. Once, I even heard them shushing my little brother (poor, confused Simon) as they crept out of the house and eased the car from the drive—leaving me, undisturbed in my sweet cocoon of freedom. I remember the first time this happened as the exact point in my life at which I felt I had finally become a normal human being, a liberated citizen of the world. Ironically, it was *education*—not religion—that had saved my life, if not my mortal soul. (Thank God for good universities!)

So, returning to the "crime" scene: There I was, all these years later, on yet another freedom-blessed Sunday, which I had, as usual, planned to stretch to near eternity: the table on my back porch already set up for my imminent brunch; Sunday's *Wall Street Journal* and June's *Harper's,* still crisply virginal in its slick, cool cover, patiently awaiting my attention; the sun wandering my garden, its warmth on my shoulders like the caress of a beloved, old friend, as I'd rock back and forth, letting my thoughts meander through the delicious morning, considering how I never tired of the birds at the feeder, the usual congregation of wrens and doves; the rowdy jay or my cardinal couple making an occasional appearance. Perhaps a blackcap chickadee would show up—or maybe a junco—jittering at the crest of my favorite hemlock, the tallest of the gracious line that runs the edge of my yard, forming the blessed barrier between my domain and that of the Cat People.

Above the maples—a shady twosome I'd grown from the seemingly impotent National Arbor Day twigs, which many years ago had arrived in the mail like a questionable gift—the sky was a wash of cerulean (the exact hue of the broken birdbath! I'd note later), still marked by the chalky thumbprint of a waxing moon. From the north, a moist breeze buffeted the maples, fluttering their leaves at me like a multitude of tiny, waving hands, as I wallowed in this bliss—when a sudden cacophony of crows rent my reverie.

The shovel jerked in my hands. Blood rushed my neck, and my gut clenched. I gave myself a shake. *Snap out of it,* I commanded my head. Time was of the essence, I knew. "Getting across the river takes building the bridge," Henry would have said. Thus, with my goal re-fixed firmly in mind, I moved toward the hemlocks, my heart knocking at every part of me.

At the exact spot where I'd aimed the shot, I stooped and pulled back the branches. Nothing. I moved a little to the right, then the left, forcing back the arms of the hemlocks as I went, to let in the light. Still nothing. I straightened up and stretched my back; and all of a sudden, I was sick to my stomach with the thought: Dear God! I must have only *wounded* Milton—or Socks! I had injured the poor, ignorant creature without killing him! Inept as I was at such warfare, I had shot him and left him to suffer, to drag himself off somewhere, to die a protracted, tortured death. My agony was complete. For a moment I went a little mad. The irony of it. The awful injustice.

Then my left-brain grabbed hold of my right. *Now is not the time for a dissertation*, I snapped at myself. I raced inside, stuffed my flashlight into the pocket of my overalls, got out the rake, lawnmower, leaf blower—basically everything I would use for any normal afternoon of yard work. On this pretense, I would scour every inch of that damn yard. I would find that damn cat.

It was about three hours later, about one o'clock, when the neighbors began their tire-screeching, door-slamming coming and going. I had searched every nook and cranny of that yard, to no avail, and had just returned to the original spot in the trees, the spot where I'd aimed the shot. The way they say a criminal returns to the scene of the crime, I remember thinking without the slightest trace of humor. Again, I pulled back the boughs and ran the beam of my flashlight into the base of that hemlock. Then I decided to rake out the gaggle of needles and leaves and trash, which somehow always finds its way in there—

And there it was! No, not the cat. A man's shoe, for God's sake! I jumped back, as though it were some dangerous, alien thing. Then before I knew what I was doing, I was picking up that shoe. I had it by the laces, holding it out before me like some exotic artifact. I remember thinking—God only knows why—that the shoe was called a "wing tip"—the oxford-tie type of shoe worn by most businessmen ("commerce clones," David called them). And I remember remarking to myself that the shoe's brown leather was worn but in quite good shape, really, which meant it couldn't have been out there very long. Not that

that was a reasonable place for a shoe, mind you. But life, as we all know, has a strange way of transporting unlikely things to unlikely places—like my car keys, which once ended up in one of the clay pots stored under the porch (fell through the floor slats).

At any rate, without actually stopping to consider cases at that point, I had the shoe by the laces, gripped in the fist of my glove. In this manner, I transported the shoe to the trash bag and dropped it in, atop the earthly debris I'd collected during my recent "yard work." I double-twisted the mouth of the bag and fastened it with one of those ratchet-type plastic ties, thinking this might help clench the stench, which, when I mowed it, emanated from my kitty-whizzed grass ("putrid poetics," David loved to call this).

The bag was still only half full—one of those outsized numbers, great for pine trimmings—so instead of putting it at the side of the house with the full ones to be put out for pickup by the borough in a few days, I pushed it, as usual, under the edge of my back porch—accessible, so I could use it yet again. (Yes, I was ecology minded long before it became fashionable.) Then, as quickly as I could, eager to get back to my *normal* life—especially what was left of my Sunday ritual (which I felt sure would reinstate my equilibrium)—I put away my tools, showered and changed, and ate an abbreviated lunch of cheddar and fruit. All the while, I forced myself not to think about what had occurred in the last twenty-four hours, not until later at least, at which time, I felt sure I would come around to beating myself up over that poor, dimwitted cat.

Well, of course, I found myself struggling with the not-thinking thing. So about three, I decided the best move was to go for my walk, and I set my sites on what we called Treadmill Hill, the grassy knoll at the other end of the neighborhood, where I'd often go to regain my sanity. Lapping the edge of the woods, I'd glide through the coolness of the tree's benevolent shadows (once you'd figured out the direction of the sun, you could mark your shade at most any time of day on that hill); listening to the multifarious birdsong; on watch for deer, redheaded flickers, yellow finches (as children, Amanda and Emily called these "wild canaries" and tried to capture them for pets); the occasional gliding hawk (yes, I know the down side of that regal creature, but *he* has no choice), and my most recent discovery: a threesome of wild turkeys, who'd raised their beady-eyed heads like submarine scopes and gawked at me, as though I were the odd-looking one.

As an added attraction, at the bottom of Treadmill Hill stood the prim, cedar-clad ranch house of Ben and Laura and baby Lotti, whose Grandpap John, when he visited, would sip his glass of port and push Lotti in her saddle swing, strung from the benevolent bough of their mighty pin oak, all the while singing to her, in his throaty baritone, choruses of "You Are My Sunshine" and "My Buddy," and, if the radio was on, he'd karaoke along with the likes of "Light My Fire" and "The House of the Rising Sun," and such. When Rachel was with me, we'd sing along with him. Mostly under our breath, but I always wondered if Grandpap John could hear us up there on his hill.

Well, after what I'd been through, Treadmill Hill seemed the singular antidote for what ailed me. And I thought I might stop by Rachel's place to see if she had yet done her daily duty. It couldn't hurt to add a sane woman's voice to the mix—not that I necessarily planned to intimate the gritty details of my debacle, although the entire scenario might have been a delectable intrigue (like one of those PBS crime shows), if I weren't the pathetic protagonist.

At any rate, my thoughts were more along the lines of the endorphin-pumping powers of the jaunt, the influx of earthly serenity for which I hoped, as the oxygen-infused air pumped though my blood and tortured brain.

And it was, in fact, just such thoughts that accompanied me, as I trotted by the Cat People's house. Just such consolation I began to savor as I glanced toward their screen door—behind which sat Milton and Socks! Wholesome and whole, wide-eyed and speculative, poised shoulder to shoulder like reigning monarchs, they peered out at me from the security of their cat domicile.

My breath caught in my throat. Then instantaneous relief swept me, and I felt such a rush of pure, sweet, innocent joy—yes, that *thrill*! I pushed my glasses back up the bridge of my nose and looked again and—yes! There they were. As large as life itself. And Heaven help me, I swear those two cats were smiling at me—arrogantly, slyly, as though they knew something I didn't.

I instantly dismissed all such thoughts. Down the street I sauntered, exhilarated, flushed with the renewed spirit of goodwill and tolerance, soaring along on the wings of *esprit de corps*, my *joie de vivre* fully back in the saddle. Pure rapture is the only way to describe how wonderful I felt as I turned back toward home—knowing those two foul creatures had escaped.

It was this joy, born of the oh-so-timely death of guilt, which carried me through the remainder of that afternoon and into the evening, as I sat on my back porch in the sweet, free air, basking in the rising glow of that gibbous moon, celebrating my rejuvenation. A repentant sinner led through the gates of Heaven.

So fully carried away was I, in fact, that when the hemlocks rustled and a squat figure emerged, muted in the darkness except for its round, white face, marked by the glow of the moon, I chose to totally and absolutely refuse to do anything but ignore it, to focus solely on the exquisite peace of the night. It was to be dismissed, I told myself, as just a slight—unintended and unremarkable—intrusion, worthy of no attention demanding no response. And I would dismiss it as such. Period.

The pistol had been secreted back to the safe, the shoe and its enshrouding trash bag under the porch and out of mind. As far as I was concerned, the matter was closed. Even when, the next day on my way back from lunch with Rachel, I could have sworn I saw—and Rachel witnessed this, too—Cat Woman scuttling back through the hemlocks from my backyard to hers, I chose to ignore it, having made the decision to, henceforth, disregard as much neighborly weirdness as humanly possible.

Irony, however, being the essence of my existence, the true core on which my earthy life turns, I should have known that it would not be that simple. Such easy peace was not to be mine.

On an evening of the following week, as I lounged in my sitting room, watching a rerun of *Cheers* (those after-dinner hours seem to beg an affable voice), a knock sounded on the steel frame of my front screen door. I jumped to turn down the sound and peeked into the foyer—a foolish grin on my face, like some kid caught with her hand in the cookie jar—to find two Whiteboro police officers on my front stoop.

They apologized for the intrusion, and we passed the necessary civilities. Then the larger of the two officers began: "Mrs. Antonelli, we have a report of . . ." The poor man was having an awful time stating his case. "If you don't mind, ma'am, could you please tell us if . . ." and, finally, he blurted it out: "Do you happen to have untended trash under your back porch?"

"Oh, God!" I gasped. My hands flew to my face. I had forgotten to put that damnable trash bag out for pickup. I'd just returned from a quick visit with Amanda for a few days, and—how embarrassing! How godawful. A bag of cat-peed grass, spoiling in the unseasonal heat. The smell back there! Just what the Cat People needed—a reason to complain about me. Again.

"I am so sorry," I said, one hand still pasted to my forehead, and hoping they wouldn't detect the scent of wine on my breath. "Yes, yes, I do, and I guess I forgot to put it out. I've been away. I'll be sure to—"

But the smaller officer cut in. "Well, ma'am," he said, shifting uneasily on his feet, "if you don't mind." He looked at his partner and then again at me. "Would you mind showing us where that is?"

Police on trash detail? I thought that seemed a bit odd, but I tucked my shirt into the top of my jeans, opened the door, and stepped outside. "Should we call in Kash Patel, do you think?' I said and grinned, but the officers seemed not in the least amused. In fact, I can't describe the way they were looking at me—actually, it was more like they were trying *not* to look at me. Their faces had become strained and distant, as though they were thinking ahead to the moment when this would be over, the way you set your mind ahead when you're doing something unpleasant or tedious, like doing taxes or giving birth. A bit melodramatic, I thought, for a mere trash event.

"Please follow me," I said with about as much sobriety as I could muster; and through the evening mist, I led them across the driveway and down the side yard, where I paused briefly to raise a hand of acknowledgment toward Horsewoman, Pony Bill, and Bull Frog, already positioned, of course, to pass whispers along the rear fence.

It wasn't until I turned the back corner of the house that the odor zapped me, and by the time we reached the back porch, I was embarrassed about to tears. I pointed the officers toward the bag, thinking how awful it was that they, in their beautiful, blue uniforms and crisp, white shirts had to deal with this.

I stood humbly aside, watching as they tugged on their latex gloves—just the way you see them do it on TV crime shows (not that I watch those mindless things). Then they gently nudged the bag forward—to get a better grasp, I supposed—and partly lifted, partly slid it from under the edge of the porch, as though it were either the most delicate or the heaviest thing they'd ever dealt with—and here, I really could not help laughing to myself, as I wondered if they were so careful with their own trash.

Instinctively, both hands clamped on my nose, as they released the tie from the neck of the bag and drew down the edges, our communal gasp erupting at the awesome stench and stunning sight before us: the insect-infested body of a man. And in the next heartbeat, I knew, without a doubt—it was Cat Man! Cat Man, all curled into himself—like one of those disgusting grubs you dig up in the garden mulch or under the grass. Cat Man, frozen in this fetalized position . . . except for his head, thrown back into the glaring beam of the officer's flashlights, to expose a ragged, swarming hole between his sightless eyes.

The universe stood still. I looked from the rigid form of Cat Man to the awestruck faces of the officers, then upward to the full-faced moon, on watch from the now dark sky.

As, from somewhere in the back of my stunned brain—perhaps in the place where the ghost of that Preacher-Bob-cursed childhood of so long ago still dwelt—a voice thundered in my head: "'Justice is mine,' sayeth the Lord."

With those awesome words echoing in my head and the shadows of those neighborly voyeurs in my peripheral vision, I looked again to the policemen, their shocked faces haloed by that luminous moon, and, God help me, the first thing that leapt from my mouth was "Holy Mother of God! Please, tell me—how many shoes does the man have on?"

The Second Wife

Liz Kelner Pozen

He fears loneliness
if I go first,
but he need not worry,
as it will go something like this:
about ten minutes after the funeral—
maybe less—
the phone will ring
or the doorbell chime
bringing comfort.
"Liz was such a lovely person," she'll say,
now all in,
the first foray over, adding
"This is a very hard time for you,
so I made a pound cake/lasagna/banana bread"
then "Why don't I come over/in
and we'll reminisce together?"
Thus it begins,
an octogenarian courtship,
abbreviated by necessity,
requiring him only to be present
and still breathing.

It's a Hard Life

Adam Archer

The kid has me by sixty pounds and six inches. Dreads pillow his massive head, which I'm tempted to tug as I reach for his cement block of a neck. I club him with my forearm, then jam my other under his shoulder and twist. His hips flip through the air and he flattens on the mat. I cinch my hold and squeeze the air out of him, deflating his ego.

"Get up," I growl, "and try to fail better." Or maybe he'll break me in half.

My wife, Mary, thinks I'm crazy, trifling with testosterone-fueled teens. She's surveyed the wreckage of my past: crisscrossed knee scars layered over metal joints, a protruding bone evidence of my dislocated shoulder. Some wounds stay unseen. My neck crunches like broken glass when it swivels. I'm half blind on my left side. Then there's the fear, never shown but grown with age—of being injured again, of failure or looking foolish. I'm old enough to be their grandfather, attempting to reclaim those gifts lost to the ravages of time.

Of which Mary reminds me on occasion. "Get up," she shouts, as if yelling will yank my flaccid phallus from senescence to tumescence, a provocation to perform. There is fear there, too, of a kind which also calls my manhood into question.

I recall the constant embarrassment, shared by others, when teenage hormones raged through me. Bored by droning teachers, we were stung to find ourselves reacting to girls in full flower bent over books and backpacks at the end of class, hard pressed to rise from our seats. Getting up was a problem because it was not a problem then. Red-faced, we'd release ourselves, regret without relief, shuffling to the door, dreading a repeat performance.

While sex was fairly frequent in the early years of our marriage, fulfilling my adolescent fantasy, the arrival of children caused the erection of careful schedules. When they got older, we'd send them out for ice cream. Mary liked banana.

As we aged and the children left the scene, however, I rarely rose to carnal occasions, which further reddened my complexion. Even then the flight wasn't long, causing Mary to comment we no longer need an egg timer. That made my blood boil but not enough. Eventually, even those precious minutes petered out and I had to confront my lack of libido. We'll lick this together, I told Mary, but she didn't want that, either.

Man plans, God laughs. Man plans a romantic evening, God laughs even harder. But such dysfunction is no laughing matter. Funny how that goes.

Hard Choices

I live in a semi-rural area, where it's said, "Men are men and sheep are scared." It's a land of lampooned liberals and alternative lifestyles. We play host to numerous new age and old age clinics, counselors, and therapies guaranteed to rejuvenate and reclaim what we've forgotten.

While I wasn't desperate, when my sex drive shifted neutral, I was willing to pursue things further if given divine direction. That came one day on the radio, with a commercial loudly touting the amazing results many men had when using acoustic wave therapy. This would, the ad boasted, repair damaged erectile tissue and boost performance. I looked up the clinic and left a message.

They called back three times in rapid succession, exhibiting more anxiety over the issue than I, and thus dropped from consideration. I was sufficiently intrigued, however, to research the therapy and the clinic's competition.

If you pay Google, you can buy ads that guarantee you appear at the top of any searches for your product or service. Since ED is a popular topic, the list of potential solution providers, replete with charlatans, opportunists, and promoters, is long. I scrolled through until I could find some serious studies with objective information. Though couched in scientific jargon, the papers were fairly straightforward. They discussed hormone therapy, testosterone supplements, shock waves, PDE5 inhibitors, vasodilation, and herbal therapy. The list goes on with multiple and overlapping potentiality from specific and combined treatments. I condensed the literature to a few pages. Now treatment was a matter of who, what, and where.

Hard Truths

Erectile dysfunction affects over 30% of men over age 40 in the United States. I don't know where they get their numbers, but it is evident I have a lot of company. There are many contributing factors: age, hypertension, smoking, drinking, stress, and genetics. Who doesn't have most of these? Then there are psychological and social components exacerbating the underlying physical conditions. I wonder how many men actually come forward to admit they've become less of a man, even to their doctor. Maybe they've lowballed the 30%.

I was inclined to disbelieve my decline, though my flagging ability to fly at even half mast was evident. I was in good physical condition, pushing myself beyond the usual boundaries of age. Still, passing 60, I suppose I had it coming. Age may be an attitude, as some say, but you can't beat it.

Hard Road Taken

When my doctor first prescribed Viagra, it was 30 bucks a pill. I jokingly asked Mary to leave some money on my pillow afterward. She was not amused. The price dropped with my performance. I went to a specialist. He prescribed Cialis, charging me 400 dollars for a 10-minute visit without an examination, which I surely would have failed. They worked once. Now I have a lot of leftover pills.

Another urologist recommended some shots, from which I literally shrank. It didn't cost much, he said, but you only have 30 days to use it once you open the package. It's good for 10 encounters. When I told Mary we would have to make love every three days to get full value from the prescription—then she was amused. "I love you," she said. "But not that much." The package remains unopened on the back shelf of our fridge.

It's embarrassing, despite its commonality. It's frustrating, because I can't, or won't, let go of the idea of who I was or what I could once do. The literature on the subject is meant to reassure, suggesting simple solutions, with cited studies biased toward the sponsor's service. Herbs, exercises, and diet changes, all augmented by natural and manufactured supplements. I tried some. They failed, since I don't live in a controlled environment or resemble a lab rat.

Doing It the Hard Way

Living in a progressive community pursuing eternal youth, it didn't take long to hook up with someone willing to pull me out of my tailspin while picking my pocket. I called to make an appointment. "We've just started our training," the woman said. "I'm booking you now but may bump you." Which she did, postponing me for a month. How much training did they need?

When the dreaded day arrived, I was given a cursory physical, followed by pages of questions to determine my qualifications for participation.

Qualification 1—Can you pay?

Qualification 2—Will you pay when it doesn't work?

Qualification 3—Will you try again and continue to pay?

Wouldn't my wife's affidavit be sufficient? Or flashing pictures of naked women to measure my response? But these were serious people who wanted serious money. Then they drew some serious blood, to see if I was seriously committed. At this point, I should have been.

They sent me home with a pile of colorful literature and a self-published book detailing what was in store. It should have come with a laugh track. The book was mostly junk, its inflated jargon and piffle easy to trim to one page, as were the "research papers." I got the picture. They would be combining myriad treatments to procure my mid-life resurrection through improved blood circulation. But now I had a team of eager sex techs wearing sanitized scrubs and rubber gloves. I felt impotent to stop the surge of well-meant intentions.

The next week, I signed more papers, my credit card having cleared. I was given more reading material, which contained the tantalizing possibility of positive side effects (bigger, thicker, healthier—the stuff of which teenage dreams are made on). They drew more blood, which, after putting it through a centrifuge, they would then directly inject into my penis. The nurse running things spoke in a matter-of-fact tone, but it was a matter of fact that I would be dropping my pants and pulling firmly on my member as they stabbed it. "Membership has its privileges" my credit card company proudly proclaimed.

Before the procedure, the nurse said I had to disinfect my penis with alcohol (*to get it drunk first?*). Then I was to slather on numbing cream and cover it with Saran Wrap while awaiting her return with a vial full of spun platelets. She entered and eyed my wrapping job.

I asked, "Am I on Candid Camera? Do you show tapes at parties?"

She ignored this and bent over me from her stool. I watched as she wiped me and plunged a blessedly short needle in several spots in my once wondrous wand. "Wait here for a few minutes while I get my equipment," she said. "Just hold it steady there."

Was this for real? I didn't know whether to laugh or cry when she left, profoundly humiliated by my predicament. The door to the room was thick enough so I couldn't hear them giggling. Even writing this now, my face flushes. At least *some* blood is moving, somewhere.

The nurse returned with a glass cylinder attached to a pressure gauge. A thin hose extended from it with a rubber bulb at the end. "This is a vacuum tube," she said. "You are going to put some lubricant all over your penis and stick it in the hole at the bottom of the cylinder."

"I am?"

"Then we're going to squeeze the bulb and inflate you inside the vacuum tube."

"So will it clean off all the dirt at the same time?"

She finally cracked a smile. "This must be a bit embarrassing for you," she said.

I recalled Hans and Franz on Saturday Night Live. "We are going to pump you up!" they shouted. They had the direction right, but the wrong muscle.

The bulb was hard to squeeze. My forearm weakened while watching my former friend grow inside the tube. I had to laugh and dropped the bulb. The nurse snatched it and started squeezing on her own. Yes, just a little embarrassing, as we watched my formerly flaccid self inflate. The stretching hurt a bit, as stretching always will when you exercise what's unused.

"Okay, we're going to do this for ten minutes. Make sure the gauge needle stays in the green zone." *Would it explode if it hit the red zone?*

The ten minutes felt like an eternity, as we alternated squeezing the bulb. By now, I was feeling dissociated from the exercise, even wishing there *was* a camera. It seemed so silly, but I reassured myself it was a "one and done" situation. The timer finally rang, the pressure released, and I yanked myself free of the cylinder. I was red from exertion and humiliation. Sweat beaded on my forehead, but at least it was over.

"Good job," she said. "Now take the apparatus home and do this twice a day for six weeks."

You want me to what? "Maybe I can sell tickets to help defray the cost," I said. "By the time I finish, I'll have forearms like Popeye. Ever hear the one about Popeye sticking it in Olive Oyl?"

She clearly hadn't but smiled anyway.

"This is just part of the therapy," she said. "Next week come back and we'll start with phase two."

Oh, goody, I thought, setting my phaser to stun.

I recounted the visit to Mary. At first her eyes grew wide in disbelief. Then she burst out laughing, which lasted until I told her the cost.

"Have you lost your mind?" she ejaculated.

Yes, among other things. "But I'm doing it for us," I said. She had no comeback. "At least the card gives us frequent flier points."

"How frequent?" she wanted to know.

That night, I locked the bedroom and bathroom doors and played with my pump.

No Hard Feelings

My protracted visit came on a Monday. On Tuesday, I went to my men's AA meeting. We get six to ten regulars there, most over 60. The intimacy of the meeting allows us to bare our souls in ways not appropriate for larger, more formal groups. Everyone shares, and our secret fears, shame and doubts are always on display.

When my turn came, I said, "Let's talk about erectile dysfunction." Some of the men instinctively crossed their legs and avoided my eyes. "I know I'm not the only one," I said, "but let me tell you what I'm doing about it." They all laughed as I related the horror of my clinical encounter. This gave me some relief, but I sensed discomfort in the room. Some shared their own experience. Clearly, I'd touched a nerve. The topic arose the following week as well, provoking mixed responses and tight smiles. We all knew. We just didn't want to say.

Going to Any Lengths

The next week was my introduction to acoustic wave therapy, the treatment that had originally impelled my investigation. I was led into a room, asked to strip, and told we (yes, we were still using the buddy system) would point a two-pound wand at various sections of my penis, which I was to pull out as far as I could. Again came the antiseptic wipe and slathered goo. Then my partner and I alternated holding the wand and stretching as we shot me full of soundwaves to repair the microcellular damage age had wrought. It was hard to keep still, and harder still to keep from sharing dick jokes with her.

A young man sees his doctor, who tells him, "You need to stop masturbating."

"Why?" the young man asks.

"Because I'm trying to examine you."

What's the difference between your jokes and your penis?
Nobody laughs at your jokes.

But she did laugh, then dropped the heavy wand on my testicles. No joke.

It Hardly Matters

The treatment was not limited to the rites of resurrection. I was given a variety of supplements: vitamins, iodine, thyroid, and something called DIM, which is how I felt. Then, for good measure, they implanted hormone pellets subdermally in my butt. I anticipated crystals and Druid chants next, but the robes remained in the closet. The pellets were supposed to give me more energy, but what I got was a sore butt.

The twice daily pumping continued. I watched comedy shows to keep my mind and eyes off "The Thing in the Tube" (not coming to a theater near you). The pills were ingested. I showed up for more wave therapy, which I could now do without assistance or an audience.

Comeuppance

I waited. Mary waited. Time wounds all heels, I thought dejectedly, as I noticed no change in my drive or the shaft that would make things go. They asked me to rate the clinic on Yelp. I gave it three yelps.

Noting Mary's growing impatience, I decided to take my buddy for a test launch. No trajectory was achieved. I remembered the unused pills and took them a few days in a row to spur myself to greater heights. I went out with a whimper, not a bang.

Back to the clinic. These things take time, the female crew assured me, then billed me for more supplements. Keep trying, they said, and let us know what comes up.

You Don't Know Dick

The therapy sessions came to an end, which was too bad considering how good I'd become at waving at least one wand in the process. Given my lack of progress on all fronts, the clinic scheduled another injection, which meant more daily dates with the tube, and another round of pellet implants. At a cost, of course. Fortunately, they knew, my credit card has no limit.

My patience does, however, but hell, why not go all the way? After all, I had nothing to lose but my dignity.

And so it goes, and so it stays, like a dog that won't come when you call.

Mary thinks my life experiences have made me hard. I wish.

In the end, I just feel I got stiffed.

A Swim in Far Rockaway

K.Z. Steel

We'd sat through weeks of classroom training. Aced the swimming pool tests. There was just one more thing standing in our way of scuba certification and, ultimately, our plan to dive in Fiji for our honeymoon: the open water dive.

Scuba trainees often complete this final stage of the certification process at their planned destination, whether it be the Caribbean, the South Pacific, or anywhere else you'd want to spend an extended period of time underwater. But my (then soon-to-be) husband, Ryan, the brains behind this scuba operation, suggested instead that we stay local and get certified during a weekend in Far Rockaway, Queens. I said sure.

What could possibly go wrong?

The site was located on a skinny strip of sand facing a channel of water separating Long Beach from the rest of Queens. Fishermen cast their lines off a small jetty and into green cloudy water littered with plastic trash. Thick yellow suds congealed in the water by the shoreline and along the jetty.

As we found parking nearby, we spotted a giant bearded bulldog of a man, sandy hair flowing behind him in the sea breeze, chain-smoking next to a beige mid-'80s model Oldsmobile. He was crammed into a skimpy black "shorty," a type of wetsuit with short sleeves and legs ending above the knee, typically worn in tropical climates. I was surprised to see someone wearing a shorty this far north, but I figured that perhaps the man's bulk would provide the necessary warmth.

"Wouldn't it be hilarious if that was our diving instructor?" I joked to Ryan.

We were about to be very amused.

His name was, aptly enough, Vinny, and he would be our dive instructor for the four certification dives we would be taking—two that day, and two the next. After brief introductions with a third dive student who'd be joining us, we wrestled into our wetsuits—Vinny included, who was covering his shorty with a more robust suit that, although visibly busting apart at the seams, he assured us was "held together with dental floss." After some unsuccessful twisting and grasping about, Vinny barked at our fellow trainee to "Zip me up!" After we were all suited up, we grabbed our equipment and headed down to the shore.

Once in the water, we would be tested on various skills. One involved the recovery of our air regulator—the mouthpiece attached to the hose connected to the air tank—should it somehow escape from our mouths. Another was the clearing of our foggy masks, which involved opening the top suction of the mask, filling it with water, then pulling out the bottom suction to empty the water. The idea was that, if an emergency were to happen 60 feet underwater, we'd have the presence of mind to calmly reach for our regulator or perform a self-induced waterboarding, instead of flailing around and praying for a quick death.

Normally, I'd avoid such dicey undertakings—I am a housecat, through and through. But Ryan insisted that scuba diving would be the "only way" to experience our honeymoon in the South Pacific.

"What's the point of going all the way down there if we can't scuba?" he asked. "What else would we even do?"

"I dunno, sightseeing?" I responded. "Relaxing on the beach? Getting blitzed on daiquiris?"

To my surprise, the scuba thing was going pretty well so far. I'd aced the skill tests in the swimming pool at St. Bartholemew's Church in midtown, where we'd taken our classroom lessons. I figured the open water dives would be no sweat.

Only in hindsight did I realize that my inflated confidence was not due to any actual skill on my part, but instead because we were surrounded by utter clowns in our scuba class. One of our fellow classmates went through the entire training process—she sat through weeks of classroom lectures, took the written exams, bought all of the scuba gear, and participated in equipment demonstrations—only to throw in the towel when it came time to swim a single lap during our final day in the pool. "I don't know how to swim," she nonchalantly explained as she packed up and left, the instructor's eyes bulging in astonishment.

During our walk down to the Far Rockaway shoreline, Vinny regaled us with a quick pep talk.

"What do you see over there?" he asked, pointing to the channel. No one spoke. We all assumed he was asking rhetorically.

But Vinny insisted, asking more aggressively this time. "What do you see over there?!" I nervously looked at Ryan, who bravely responded.

"Uh, water?"

"Nope." Vinny forcefully shook his head. "I don't see the water." Dramatic pause. "I see what's *under* the water. You know how I know? Because I've *been there*."

Vinny then plunged his meaty hand into the opaque water at the shoreline, fished around for a moment, and held up a rotted, slime-covered rope that descended ominously into the murky depths. He instructed us to grab onto the rope and follow it underwater until we reached a cage at the bottom. "Hang on to the cage," he said, "and we'll do our tests there."

We put our blind trust in Vinny, ignoring all five of our senses and any shred of basic reasoning. We obediently flipper-marched into the water like bewildered penguins, grabbing the rope as we went: the other trainee first, then Ryan, then me. Vinny followed behind.

As I submerged myself under the muck, a plastic drinking straw plunked into my mask. Once underwater, I could barely see more than a foot in front of me. Lower and lower, deeper and deeper I went, until finally I felt my flippers sink into the mushy ocean floor.

A rickety setup vaguely materialized before me. I started to panic. Was this the cage Vinny mentioned? Where did everybody else go? Is that Ryan over there? Did I get lost? What if I get stuck down here? What if I *die* down here, amidst the scuzz and ooze? I was nearly hyperventilating, a suboptimal situation while several yards underwater and relying on a limited supply of air from a tank.

A large figure eclipsed what little light streamed through. Vinny. I gave him a thumbs-up sign—which, in scuba speak does not mean "I'm cool" but instead means "I must surface. *Now!*" Vinny shook his head and flashed a thumbs-down, like a deranged Joaquin Phoenix in *Gladiator*, and actually shoved me down to make his point. Normally, I'd be cowed into submission by the social pressure to be polite, but fear and outrage prevailed. I refused to be bullied by this bewetsuited behemoth. I wrenched away and bolted upwards. Vinny followed.

"What's going on?" he bellowed once we were at the surface. I explained how I freaked out when I got to the cage because I couldn't see anything. I just couldn't do it.

Vinny sighed. "Look, if you want to go back, that's fine. I'll bring you to shore. You wouldn't be the first to quit. But you've done all this work, spent a ton of money, you should follow through. I won't judge you if you go back. But you'll regret it if you don't finish." A bodega plastic bag floated by, its yellow smiley face half-submerged.

He was right. So back into the sludge I went, slowly sinking down to the death cage, where I joined two hazy figures, presumably Ryan and the other student diver. Vinny swam to one of them to begin the test. From what I could make out, Vinny pantomimed a scuba skill, and the diver imitated said skill. Rinse and repeat, with all the other skills. Then, the figures merged, followed by a burst of commotion—flailing arms and air bubbles shooting everywhere—which went on for some time.

Hm, I thought. I didn't recall this last part happening at the St. Bart's pool. But any sense of self-preservation was overruled by my desperation to avoid another motivational speech from Vinny. So I did what any sane cult follower would do: I convinced myself that this was totally normal. "Just like the pool," I reassured myself. Just like the pool.

The testing was then repeated with the second diver: Vinny pantomiming skills, the diver repeating them, capped off by a bunch of explosive activity.

It was now my turn. Here we go. Vinny instructed a skill, and I complied. Clearing my mask. Check. Recovering a lost regulator. Check. I had this in the bag.

Vinny then grabbed my dive vest with one hand and used his other hand to jam the button on my regulator—yes, that regulator, the one right next to my face—sending bubbles everywhere. I was somehow shocked by this—How could Vinny betray me like this? He was so *nice*!—despite witnessing him do this very same thing with the other divers. Twice. By instinct, I tried swimming away to escape the situation, but Vinny wasn't having it. He yanked me back down. Resigned to my fate, I rag-dolled into submission. After 45 minutes (okay, more like 30 seconds) of this, Vinny let go, abandoning the effort of trying to murder me.

Vinny later disclosed to us that "the old regulator trick" was a way of demonstrating that a diver could still breathe underwater even if his or her regulator got stuck. An effective, if extremely violent, way to make a point.

After the testing phase, Vinny motioned for us to follow him on an underwater boondoggle. And follow him we did. By that point any remaining survival instincts had long vanished. We were in Vinny's world now. We puttered around aimlessly.

Where were we going? *Who knows?*

Which way was up? *Who cares?!*

Did I have enough air? *Shrug*.

I'd long stopped caring about such pesky details, confident that if I went astray, Vinny would be all over me like a cheap wetsuit. And just then it appeared before me: a bright light shining from the tunnel of darkness. I was euphoric as I inched closer and closer to it, knowing that it was now time to shed my mortal coil and exit this world for the next.

I then emerged at the water's surface. Confused, I lifted my mask, blinked a few times, and looked around.

I made it! I was alive!

I marveled at all of the sights, sounds, and smells that seemed so much more saturated than before. The sky shimmered in a cerulean blue that I'd never before noticed. The warmth of the sun—oh, the bright shining sun!— enveloped me like a portly grandmother's embrace. The cigarette butts danced like angels atop the waves gently lapping the shore.

But my triumph, like the original stitching on Vinny's wetsuit, was short-lived.

"You guys ready to do this again in a few hours?" Vinny asked as we made our way to shore.

I froze. My stomach dropped. I had totally forgotten—we had three more dives to go.

"Well," Vinny chuckled, "since that was way rougher than anything you're going to see in Fiji or wherever, what do you say we just call it a day?"

Ryan, the other diver, and I exchanged confused looks. Then it dawned on us.

"Yes," Vinny confirmed. "You're done for the weekend. You are now certified. Congratulations."

We then drove over to the local Dunkin' Donuts, where we celebrated our victory, endured several more of Vinny's scuba war stories, and doctored up our dive books to record the three phantom dives. In exchange, Vinny demanded two Boston cream donuts and an extra-large iced coffee, extra light, extra sweet.

That seemed like a fair trade.

Early Man

Richard D. Key

It's the dawn of civilization and we've managed to catch our proto-protagonist and his mate having a discussion in the stony cavern they call home. Some would call it a squabble.

"Why did you let the fire go out?" he demands, having mastered some sort of basic communication.

"I thought that was your job," she replies, not to be bested in the art.

"How do you expect me to tend the fire when I'm out hunting and gathering all the freakin' day? Huh?"

"Well, how am I supposed to do it when I'm stuck in this cave taking care of kids all the freakin' day? Huh?"

"That's another thing. Why do you keep having babies? You've had like eight or nine already. Isn't that enough?"

"I think you know what happens."

"That's just it. I *don't* know! I *don't* know! It seems you just like having babies. Stop already!"

"Honestly?"

"I come home from a hard day of killing things and trying to provide. Then I have to spend what time's left tending the fire like I'm some kind of pyromaniac. I'd like to have some free time for a change. Some *me* time."

"Oh, that's rich. When do *I* get some me time?"

There's a pause in their discussion, a moment of blessed silence except for the wild yelps and shrill echoes of unknown creatures crying in the distance. Then she continues.

"Nick the Neanderthal says life's a bitch and then you die."

"Nick the Neanderthal, Nick the Neanderthal. That's all I ever hear. Nick, Nick, Nick. I don't like Nick. Last week I saw him slinking around here, and he looked at me with this smug this-is-my-territory kind of look."

"Nick's sweet. He brings me presents."

"Well, I don't like Nick. I hate Nick. Next time I see him around here I'm going to knock his brains out."

"He's twice your size."

"I'll climb a tree and jump on him! Then I'll knock his brains out. That'll teach him!"

"You should probably go borrow some fire from the neighbors. It's getting cold."

"All right. But next time it goes out, don't come crying to me. We'll just freeze to death."

Our protagonist heads out into the cold with a club-like torch and returns with it glowing, sparks flying into the darkness. Once the fire is going strong and the walls of the cave begin to glow, he squats, mesmerized by the flames, deep in contemplation.

"Just one day I'd like to do something fun. Just one day."

"Fun? What does that even mean?"

"I don't know. The other day I saw Dirk—you know Dirk, red hair, kind of chubby."

"Yes."

"Dirk was in the meadow by himself knocking a white ball around with a stick. He was having the best time."

"A stick?"

"Yeah. Just an ordinary stick."

"And then what?"

"Well, he'd hit the ball and try to get it into a hole."

"And then what?"

"If he got it into a hole then he'd take it out and try to hit it into another hole. It looked like fun."

"That's the dumbest thing I ever heard."

"Well, I'd like to try it someday. If I ever had the time. Of course, I never will."

"Maybe it'd make more sense to try pulling a fish out of the water. At least then we'd have something to eat."

"Is that all you think about? Eat, eat, eat? There's more to life than eating."

"Like starving? Starve, starve, starve. I think about that, too. Here's an idea. Why don't you try inventing something that would make our lives better? You used to be creative, back when we first met."

"Well, as a matter of fact I was thinking the other day about the wheel. I don't want to re-invent it or anything. But, I'm sure I could make it better."

"See! That's what I mean."

"Here's what I was thinking. I was thinking about getting three wheels and attaching them together somehow. And you know what I would call it?"

"No."

"A triceratops."

"Triceratops? That name's taken. Those large beasts with the three horns?"

"Well in that case I'll call it . . . the thing with three wheels. It could be amazing. Then people would bring me furs and pelts and food in exchange for the thing with three wheels. I could stay here and help with the kids. And the older ones could help put the things with three wheels together. I don't know. Maybe I'm a dreamer."

"We all have dreams. I'd like to go on a long walk someday. Leave all the kids with Mom and Dad. Just head off and follow the river to see where it goes. Nick says there's wide, wide water not too far away."

"There you go again! Nick this, Nick that! And, by the way, your parents couldn't take care of a turtle. They are worn out. *Totally* worn out. They're ancient! They're almost *forty* for Gosh sakes!"

"Why don't you take us to see that cave you talk about, the one with all the pictures on the wall. We could all use a little culture."

"Yeah. I suppose we could do that. I've heard things have changed since when I was a kid, though. It's not free anymore. You have to give them something in return. And there's all sorts of signs up. Don't touch the paintings. No dogs allowed. No flash photography."

"What does *that* mean?"

"Who knows? It's just rules, rules, rules. What's the use in being a caveman if you have to follow rules all the time?"

"That reminds me. We got a note from the neighborhood cave owners association."

"What do *they* want?"

"They say the outside of our cave isn't up to the standards outlined in the bylaws. We have one month to make changes or we'll have to leave."

"For crying out loud! I've had it with those control freaks! I'd like to bash their brains in!"

With that, he goes on a rampage around the cave throwing rocks at random targets and bashing the fire with a club until sparks are flying everywhere and three babies are crying.

"See what you've done? You've upset the children! You've got to stop being so aggressive! If you want to live with other humans and closely related species you need to learn to keep your emotions in check. I know you don't want to hear this, but Nick says no man is free who cannot control his emotions."

"That's it! Why don't I just go get Nick right now and tell him to take my place? Huh? Would that make you happy to have Mr. Perfect Nick the Neanderthal right here with you day after day? Is that what you want?"

Well, that is exactly what she got. Our protagonist abandoned his cave-dwelling family, and Nick moved in the following week. Nick, true to his nature, fixed up the cave entrance to a T and later himself joined the cave owners association, which elected him chairman.

Sadly, the thing with three wheels never took off, and our protagonist became disillusioned with the invention process, family life, and prehistoric existence in general. But that is not to say he didn't leave something for posterity. He got himself a set of sticks and joined Dirk in the meadow, day after day, knocking the white balls into the holes, until one day it took seven tries to get the white ball into the hole and he snapped. From the front of the cave he used to call home, he could just be seen in the valley below, tossing his sticks hither and yon, breaking some in half and others into multiple pieces. He gave up the game he learned from Dirk and swore he'd never set foot in the meadow again. But because of his daring (and selfish) me-time misadventure, the world was gifted the concept of the triple bogey meltdown.

Animal Husbandry

Aili Whalen

It all started on vacation in a tiny country named Xingoux halfway across the world from our house in Dayton, Ohio, that was once part of French Polynesia and that was now (somehow) independent. My wife, Anne, chose Xingoux after I forbade her from stalking the local no-kill animal rescue's adoption pages. We had just lost our longtime golden retriever, Millie, and I didn't think we should get a rebound pet based on knee-jerk grief alone. I was a little bit worried about our marriage during times of trouble, to be honest, since Anne sometimes had long-lasting depressive episodes that were triggered by sad events. During these times she would act impulsively, erratically, and the fallout from these actions could sometimes have longer implications than did the original triggering event. Once we ended up the temporary co-owners of a wool sheep, for example, when Anne tried to stanch the pain of yet another miscarriage by throwing herself into knitting. That had led to wanting to card and dye her own wool. And that had led us to a failing sheep farm near Yellow Springs, Ohio, that Anne had to save.

"Well, I have to look at some cute animals, Jerry," Anne said. "I just have to. How about if I Google 'cutest rare animal in the world' so we can be sure there isn't one at the local shelter?"

Before I could reply, she had done the Googling and up popped a Chouchou's smiling, furry little face. It was about the size and shape of an Australian quokka, with a cuddly body, big-cheeked face, and perky ears. It also had the charcoal-colored four-fingers and one-thumb hands of a bonobo and larger, furry arms that looked like a sloth's.

"Look at this!" Anne gasped.

"That really is adorable," I agreed too quickly, comforting myself that at least there weren't any close to us—the nearest Chouchou was on an island on the other side of the world. Too remote, I thought stupidly, for us to visit.

Unfortunately, the damage had already been done. Every waking thought (and some dreaming ones too) that didn't center on Millie, gorgeous, sweet Millie whom we missed so much, was fixated on photos and videos of Chouchous.

"What harm could it do," Anne said one night with tears in her eyes, "to just visit them in Xingoux?"

I said nothing.

Anne doubled down. "Do I really ask you for that much, Jerry?" she asked. "I just want to go on a vacation. We're retired and we have plenty of money. I just want to see the Chouchous. What is so wrong with that?"

Nothing is wrong with that, I thought. Except that I knew that Anne's obsessions, her loves, her passions, often did have a way of going down a rabbit hole and taking me with her. It was one of the things I loved about Anne when the rabbit hole turned out to be just the place I wanted that I didn't know I had always wanted (like rescuing Millie, a starving, plaintive pup on the side of the road).

"Would you like to meet some of our Chouchous?" a sanctuary guide asked. "This is not a zoo, after all. Our laws are very progressive here. Chouchous, as perhaps you know, are very intelligent and sensitive beings. As such, they have been given some rights on par with that of a human being."

"Is that so?" I asked. At the time, the full meaning of this did not register with me.

Once in the enclosure, one Chouchou bounded right up to Anne and leaped into her arms.

"Oh, Jerry, how adorable!" Anne exclaimed. The Chouchou put its little hand on her shoulder and gazed into her eyes.

"That's Hazel," the guide explained. "She's taken a shine to you."

"Who's this?" I asked. There was another, slightly larger Chouchou with a black marking on its face that looked like a mustache who was sitting at my feet and cutting his eyes at me. Then he did something that I could swear looked like a wink. "Waka waka waka," it said in a tone that could be translated as "hey, there, how ya doin'?"

"That's Herbert. Her brother. They are fraternal twin three-year-olds, which in human years is twenty-one."

"Can I pick him up?" I asked.

"No need." The guide laughed.

Herbert quickly and nimbly climbed my leg and settled himself on my back with his furry arms around my shoulders.

"He feels like a hiking backpack!" I exclaimed.

"Would you like to take them for a walk?" the guide asked.

We did. That day, Anne and I took Hazel and Herbert for a walk and found them to be delightful company. Hazel had a way of humming gentle little vibrant melodies along the way. And Herbert would point at various trees and flowers that we passed and mutter his sound-effect commentary. The trees were abundant with coconuts, breadfruit, and leafy shade. There were white gardenias and pink and orange frangipani.

If I seemed to understand him, and translated what I thought he meant in English, Herbert would give me a high-five. If he wanted me to try again, he would shake his head no.

Hazel was less verbal but more expressive with her eyes and hands. She would put one hand on Anne's cheek or stroke her hair to show affection and empathy.

We started coming back every day to visit the Chouchous and go on walks or (longer) hikes. Occasionally, during lunch or other rest breaks from walks or hikes they would disappear behind a tree and whisper (Herbert) and make touch signals on his chest or arm (Hazel) together. We didn't follow them, or demand to know what they were talking about (we have some social sense after all and believed that it was good for them to understand, in return, when Anne and I needed privacy), but it did remind us that they had a long-standing relationship that preceded their meeting us. Just like my and Anne's relationship, I guess. Except now Hazel had an influence on Anne too.

"Anne, what would you think if we went back to the hotel now for some lunch and came back later?" I would ask.

Hazel would instantly start stroking Anne, after which Anne would reply coolly, "There is plenty of food here in the cafeteria. There is no need to go back."

I started to associate the Hazel strokes with my not getting to do what I wanted.

But Anne was so happy. Happier than I had seen her since Millie passed. Her skin, which had started looking gray, had color back in it now. She smiled. She laughed.

I was also quite enjoying my relationship with Herbert, which felt kind of like a caddie one on the golf course. He would not only point out interesting things to look at on our way but would jump down to clear some branches in our path or steer us clear of a bug-infested area. I started to rely on Herbert even to guide our walking altogether, and it was nice not having to be the compass of the family for a change.

The Chouchous were not like the wool sheep. They weren't difficult and bleaty and resistant. Overall, they were well-trained to be adaptable to our needs. When we stopped walking on our hike, they scrambled down, sat at our feet, and waited patiently for the next instruction, like well-trained Boy Scouts. If Herbert wanted to take one path and me another, he would gesture in a way that seemed to say, "After you." But since his guidance was more experienced as to the terrain, I started to do what he suggested by feel of which way he wanted to go from his body language. I was the horse to his rider perhaps.

All of this felt great for both me and Anne and was enjoyable. The more we sort of fell into reliance on the Chouchous, though (Anne for Hazel's strokes and me for Herbert's guidance), the more a sort of queasy feeling started in my stomach. It felt kind of like the feel of a soft undertow in an unknown ocean. I tried to Google Chouchous, and Xingoux, but then remembered that one of the benefits of Xingoux that they prided themselves on was being completely off the grid. There was no WiFi or cellular service that tourists could use—all of the communication services they had were for island businesses and naturalized citizens. "Not to worry," our hotel concierge had said. "That's what I am here for. You need anything, you come to me."

"What's wrong with spending our vacation time enjoying some cute, cuddly animals and being outside in the fresh air?" Anne asked, sensing my growing discomfort.

What indeed?

On the sixth day we woke up to find that we both were missing the Chouchous fiercely.

"This is getting ridiculous!" Anne explained.

"Yes, I know!" I laughed. "But I can't seem to help myself. And they seem to like us too, although since their tails don't wag like dogs' it's hard to tell." The Chouchous' tails were more like sloth tails—short and stubby. The affections Hazel showed Anne were the gazes and pats. The affection Herbert showed me was a sort of man-hug—a pressure or pat on the back or nod of encouragement. Sometimes Hazel and Herbert walked together far ahead of or behind us with their heads together (again, Hazel patting Herbert, Herbert whispering in his own language), and their hips or shoulders would bump companionably. But mostly when we were all together Hazel stuck to Anne and Herbert to me.

By the last day of our vacation (we had been there for ten days) we found it hard to leave. Not just for the usual reasons, that we had lives and friends and families back in the States, but because we had become attached to the Chouchous.

"What if . . ." Anne said tearfully.

"No, Anne!"

"Now just hear me out. What if we asked about adoption? The sanctuary seems overrun with Chouchous. Perhaps it would lessen the burden on them if two were given a good home?"

I paused for a moment. The Chouchous weren't dogs, after all. But we had been around them enough now to see that they weren't difficult at all. They ate mostly fruit and nuts. They used a designated area to go to the bathroom. They slept at night and were awake during the day like human beings. There were also clean and didn't bite.

"Well," I said. "I'm not saying I agree that it's a good idea. But it couldn't hurt to get a bit more information, just in case."

"Just in case!" Anne said, laughing. "I'll take it!"

Just in case is what I had said before we adopted Millie. While we were waiting for Millie to be healthy enough to be put up for adoption, we had agreed to foster her *just in case* she needed us to get well. One day I was reading in my favorite chair and Millie came and leaned against me before putting her big head on my lap. After looking into those soft brown eyes, I was done for. "Foster fail!" Anne had said gleefully.

"**We have to do** *what* to take Herbert and Hazel out of the country?"

"Marry them," Bob, the Xingoux sanctuary guide said.

"Is Bob your real name?" I had asked. "No," he said. "But it's easiest for tourists to say and remember." All of the hotel workers and guides on the island had names like this. The men were Bob or John. The women were Sue or Jane.

"Why do they have to be married?" I asked. "Is it to ensure they stay together?"

"They don't need to stay together."

"Then . . . ?"

"I think you are misunderstanding. They don't need to be married to each other." Bob shuffled some papers on his desk. "They need to be married to YOU."

"What?" Anne and I said in unison.

"To you," Bob repeated. "Each adult person can marry one Chouchou according to our laws. And the only way a Chouchou can leave the country is with a lawful spouse. That way we don't have to track them down and bring them back if you decide you want to keep them."

"We want to keep them but as PETS," Anne insisted.

"Not possible. Their rights are equivalent to human rights," Bob explained. "They cannot be kept as pets."

"But we're already married!" I exclaimed.

"You have Chouchou spouses already?" the guide said. "Why didn't you say so?"

"We're married to each other, and our country doesn't allow bigamy!"

"Now, now," Bob said. "If your country doesn't acknowledge marriage between a human and an animal then surely an out-of-country marriage to a Chouchou can't be bigamy."

My wife and I were too flummoxed to respond.

"Well, I'm not sharing Jerry with Hazel," Anne said wryly. "And I'm certainly not letting him consummate a marriage with someone else."

"No worries," Bob said. "This is a very common misgiving. No physical consummation is needed—we only require a communion of souls. Also, Jerry need not marry Hazel. You can."

Anne looked at me helplessly.

"Gay marriage is not a problem in Xingoux either," Bob explained. "As I said earlier, we are a very progressive country."

"And to get Herbert as well?"

Everyone looked at me.

"I can marry Herbert?"

"Well, yes," Bob said.

"I think we're out of luck, honey," I said.

"Because you're a homophobe?" Anne retorted.

"No! Because I won't marry an animal when I'm already married!"

"A marriage that doesn't have to be consummated!"

"Ah, but it does," Bob repeated. "You have to have a communion of souls. Hazel and Herbert have to agree to be married to you."

"They have to . . . ?"

"We have a sign for that that we have taught them," Bob said, "since we train all Chouchous to one day be married to humans and their consent is a necessary part of this as I have said. Shall we ask them?"

"No, no, no, no, no," I said.

Anne looked furious. "I'm not leaving Xingoux without Hazel and Herbert," she said.

"I guess we'll be staying here a while then," I said weakly.

"At least three months," Bob said. "That's the minimum waiting period and over the course of the three months the Chouchous have to sign their consent multiple times."

We stayed three months. I stayed under protest. Anne stayed out of pure stubbornness. And in the meantime, our dependence on and need to be with the Chouchous only grew stronger. Anne claimed that she couldn't sleep without Hazel's pats, so I had to try to imitate them for her. And when I was away from Herbert, I felt a bit helpless, lost even, without my trusty guide. Hazel and Herbert signed their consent to marry us almost immediately, as if they were expecting this. After three months of repeated signing somehow, wildly and improbably, with me telling myself that it was just a foreign formality, we did, indeed, marry them under the laws of Xingoux.

We found two small airline-approved dog carriers that would allow the Chouchous to fit nicely under the seats in front of us. All went smoothly at the Xingoux airport, and the flight home was easy.

Then we hit US Customs.

"What are these? Livestock?" the Customs agent asked. "Exotic pets?"

"Exotic pets!" we said, relieved.

"Pet adoption papers?" The agent put out his hand.

I handed him our marriage certificates. He glanced through them quickly. "Pet adoption papers?" he repeated.

"It's a funny thing," I said. "Xingoux won't let you adopt a Chouchou, so we don't have pet adoption papers. They make you marry them instead—treating the Chouchou as someone with rights equivalent to a human person—but, really, they will be pets."

"You're telling me you're married to these animals?"

"Yes," I said, my face reddening. "As a technicality. Not a real marriage, of course. They will be pets."

"A fake marriage."

"A technically real marriage."

"Sir, it can't be a real marriage for purposes of entry to the United States because the US doesn't recognize interspecies marriages. No pet adoption papers, no entry."

"We can't enter our own country?"

"Not with those two Chouchous you can't."

"We can enter without them?"

"No, we can't take the Chouchous—you'll have to go back to Xingoux and return them. Or . . ." he said.

"Or?"

"Or we can keep them here in quarantine—for a fee—until you get your pet adoption papers in order. The normal quarantine time is six months for exotic pets. But I can expedite the process for a surcharge that we can negotiate."

"Jerry, I'm not leaving them here!" Anne grabbed my sleeve. "I will not leave them here!"

"So, what are we supposed to do? Go back to Xingoux?"

Anne grabbed the bag with Herbert in her left hand (Hazel was in the bag in her right) and glared at me.

We went back to Xingoux. And back to the Chouchou sanctuary. Herbert and Hazel leapt out of our arms and into their favorite leaf-munching trees as soon as we were there. Bob, a different guide with a Bob nametag—our original guide no longer worked there, it seemed—looked not at all surprised when we updated him on our story. This angered me.

"Why did your sanctuary send us on that fool's errand and make us marry the Chouchous?" I demanded. "You must have known the US wouldn't allow us entry!"

"We knew no such thing," Bob 2 said coolly. "US laws change constantly. Who am we to keep up? You are the ones who are traveling, and it's your responsibility to know what you can and can't do vis-à-vis your own country."

"We want an annulment," I said evenly.

"Certainly," Bob 2 said. "You can have an annulment provided that it's within forty-eight hours of your marriage. Let me just see . . . Uh oh. It's been over three days. No annulment is possible."

"Then give us pet adoption papers that the US will accept, and we'll call it a day."

"I can't do that."

"Why not?"

"As we explained many months ago," Bob 2 looked at me as if I were a wayward child, "Chouchous are not pets in Xingoux. They have human-level rights."

"We'll see you in court!" I shouted.

"All right," Bob 2 said without missing a beat. "Where are you going?"

"We're leaving to find a lawyer!"

"You can't leave Herbert and Hazel here."

"Why not?"

"They don't belong here anymore. They are married to you and Anne, and as such they are your responsibility. This sanctuary is only for unmarried Chouchous without a human spouse protector."

"If they have human rights, don't they have the right to live independently?"

"No, they don't. They have human rights at the level of not being pets but not enough rights to be fully independent. They need spousal guardians. The law is plain. You can read it yourself. When you consult your lawyer."

We left with Herbert and Hazel and brought them back to our hotel. To our surprise there were no issues with signing them in with our marriage certificates. Indeed—and why had we not noticed this before?—there were other Chouchous accompanying human beings in the lobby, in the dining area, and by the pool.

We consulted a Xingoux lawyer named John who specialized in international and immigration law.

"Can you help us to get a pet adoption license the US will accept? Can we travel to Paris or something and get the Chouchous licensed as exotic pets and THEN go to the US?"

"No," John said. "There aren't any other countries that will give you the pet adoption license you seek because everyone knows that Chouchous come only from Xingoux. And you can't get an annulment because you're past the time limit for annulment. The best you can do to get out of this is divorce."

"Divorce?" I said hopefully. "I'll take a divorce!"

"I won't!" Anne said. "Jerry, I'm not leaving these Chouchous. If you divorce Herbert, I still won't divorce Hazel, and Hazel and I will live happily in Xingoux forever."

"There is a nice ex-pat community here," John said. "Especially because Xingoux is a Community Property country. If you divorce a Chouchou, they get half of your net worth. Unless you have a prenup?"

"A PRENUP?!" I yelled.

"Don't yell at me. You're the one who got married to a Chouchou without knowing what you were doing and without getting a prenup. Fat chance you'll get a postnup now."

I looked at Herbert and Hazel. They were smiling. And both shaking their heads no.

My Sprung Zipper

Geoffrey K. Graves

My entire wedding's a blur because all I could think about was the zipper on my rent-a-tux pants hopelessly snagged in the open-for-business position. It would not budge. I couldn't ask my fiancée to fix it because you're not supposed to see the bride before you're wed, and my ex–best friend Jerry, who was also my ex–best man, was no help because he'd totally flaked out for what he said was a family emergency that turned out to be an NBA playoff game on television at our usual watering hole. I turned to my future brother-in-law, who I'd just met, to give me a hand with the zipper.

"You want me to help you do what to your what?" he asked, and I re-explained my predicament.

"Stuck, in the open-for-business position, huh?" he said. "I don't mind helping out so long as you make sure the salesman doesn't make an appearance in the, uh, doorway."

At first John seemed like one of those take-charge kind of guys who are good in situations like this, but that was before he used the pliers from his truck toolbox to give the zipper pull tab a strong yank that snapped off said tab resulting in a bloody nose for John when the pliers backlashed and whapped him in the face. We were in the officiating priest's office. I had to stop John from reaching for the priest's vestments to blot the blood gush that eventually took half the box of Kleenex to stanch. He stuffed plugs up his nostrils to stop the schnoz from oozing.

“Sorry about dat,” he honked, now sounding like he had a bad cold. “I really tawt dat wood get da job dun.” Next, John tried sealing up the opening with a large patch he fashioned from scotch tape found in another drawer. The tape was lying next to a bottle of whiskey from which he took a generous belt.

When he picked up a magic marker with which I guess he was going to color the tape in an attempt at camouflage, I said, “Hold on, Picasso. This isn’t going to work.” I was right. The patch gaped apart after one test step. It didn’t help that the pants were a lot tighter than they should have been, which was my fault. I’d committed to losing a few—I guess it was ten—pounds before the happy day, but that didn’t happen.

John next pulled out a stapler from a drawer, and I said, “Whoa, whoa, whoa. You’ve got to be kidding.” After he nipped a second slug of the priest’s Jameson, John told me to hold still because we were running out of time, which I did, very still, because I could tell the whiskey had already kicked in and he wasn’t being very careful and to put it bluntly I didn’t want my dick stapled to my leg.

After his third slurp of booze, which I emphatically but unsuccessfully tried to discourage, John nailed the two sides of the talon zipper with a bajillion staples. Everything held, but the shiny silver staples made my crotch look like a Goth teen with multiple piercings, so I hiked my cummerbund down a lot lower than its traditional location. The bottom of your average cummerbund typically lines up at the top of the pants zipper, but to disguise the situation that’s where the top of my cummerbund lined up, the bottom coming in well below the fun zone twins. I looked like Chiquita Banana ready to dance the rhumba. It wouldn’t have been so noticeable had I got the black cummerbund that came standard with the rental, black on black blending nicely together, but me being Mister Snazzy, who must have been feeling patriotic that day, paid extra for a combo set they called the Old Glory, an American flag job with matching star-spangled clip-on bow tie. John, who decided he was a comedian, started saying the Pledge of Allegiance to my crotch.

"And to da re-pubic for which it stands—"

"Yeah, yeah," I interrupted. "You keep fiddling around down there, and the re-pubic just might start standing up."

"One nation, under balls, indivisible . . ."

The ceremony began, and after I walked up to the altar and turned around, my mother in the front row kept signaling me to pull up my cummerbund. I did my best to telepathically communicate that I couldn't. Then Jennifer came waltzing down the aisle doing that stutter step thing with her father and both gave me a dubious up-and-down as they approached.

"And who gives away this woman to this man?" the priest asked, looking toward Jennifer's father and shocking me because while Jennifer and I wanted a traditional wedding, Jennifer specifically made clear that old-fashioned question was to be eliminated. I agreed, it harkening to the days when a young woman was seen as her father's property like his cattle.

Now panicked, I looked over at Jennifer, who is as strong-willed as a woman can be, something I admire in her. She winked at me and pronounced quite emphatically, "I do."

The women in the church whooped and applauded enthusiastically as did most men a beat behind their ladies, while Jennifer's father took the opportunity to whisper in my ear that I needed to pull up my cummerbund, "Because it's way too low."

I whispered back, "No can do. Zipper's broke." An ex-Marine, he gave a sharp military nod, sat in the front row of the bride's side, and had an animated back-and-forth with his wife, who wound up smiling. Then he started smiling. I could tell they were discussing the cummerbund issue. The way they were stifling their giggles, I thought the two of them were going to crack, and by the tension on their faces they were pretty close.

The minister began the ceremony like this: "Elliot Johnson and Jennifer Evans have invited all of you dear folk to witness this most special day of their lives." He was wearing one of those headset microphones pop singers wear because it was a big church full of people, and between that sentence and the next he cupped his hand over the microphone and whispered, "Pull up your cummerbund. It's slipped down."

"Zipper's broke," I side-mouthed, which brought a slow smile to his face he did his best to suppress. Then from the front pew on the groom's side, my mother started intensely chatting with my father, who seemed to have intuited the situation correctly and discreetly pointed at his crotch and then in my crotch's direction, which brought a broad grin to my mother, which she covered with her hand while my father blurted out a chortle but tried to cover it with a cough. To recap, the Evanses were both smiling one of those can't-stifle-it smiles, the same for my folks, and ditto for Father Riley. Even Jennifer's bridesmaids had caught the smiling fever. Jennifer was not smiling.

At that point I knew I had to do something, so I leaned into the clergyman's microphone and said, "Just so everybody knows, my zipper broke. John stapled it shut and that's why my cummerbund is so low." I thought that would quell the situation, but the entire church erupted in laughter. Uproarious, totally unnecessary laughter. John stood and took a bow for saving the day, finishing up with an aggressive fist pump and an enthusiastic "Woo-hoo," that somehow caused both yucky nose plugs to rocket out onto the bosomy lady sitting beside him, who turned out to be Jennifer's favorite aunt.

"What the hell, John!" she exclaimed, looking like she'd escaped from the movie *Carrie*.

"Now, I have to pee very badly," I continued into the microphone as calmly as possible, provoking more laughter, which was not my intention. "And it's going to take me a while to get out of these pants because they've been stapled to my underwear." More ridiculous laughter. Much more than the situation required.

"Oh, God. *I'm* going to pee *my* pants," Terry Ann, Jennifer's matron of honor, said, snorting in unbridled hilarity. Clearly, something had to be done.

I held up my hands to take charge of the situation, waiting until the laughter simmered down to a light tittering. "Therefore," I said, as somberly as I could, "if we could get on with the ceremony, that would be great."

That's when Jennifer surprised everyone by throwing her little wrist bouquet at me and stormed up the aisle. "You always have to make a joke out of everything, Elliot."

"So, my ex-best friend Jerry, I hope that answers your question as to why I'm here in the Hair of the Dog, sitting next to you on a barstool in my rented tuxedo with the broken zipper and American flag cummerbund situated way too low watching the Lakers game and drinking a Jack and coke."

"Okay. But why's Terry Ann here, and what's she doing in the bathroom?"

"Well, like I said, she really had to pee, and I guess the church bathroom was occupied so she ran over here."

"Anything else interesting happen?"

"Yeah. Terry Ann farted."

"How romantic. In the middle of the ceremony?"

"Yeah. Actually, a lot of farts. Like a machine gun. When she ran off to pee, she ripped out a whole series of them. Brought the house down."

"Dammit, I always miss the good stuff."

"She's probably embarrassed. Hang on, I'm getting a text. It's Jennifer. She wants me to come back to the church."

"Oh. Hunh. You gonna go?"

"Of course, I'm going, Jerry. It's my wedding day."

"She still wants to marry you?"

"Looks like it. And don't sound so surprised."

"You, er, don't want me to come with you, do you?"

"Nah. You've already irredeemably trashed your reputation. No reason to try and salvage it at this point. Catch up with us after at the reception once everyone's had a chance to get appropriately anesthetized." I stood up.

"You're the best friend this ex–best friend ever had, Elliot. I'd hug you if it wasn't for, you know, your zipper situation."

"Speaking of which," I said, "trade pants with me."

"What!"

"You heard me. You owe me."

"Shit," Jerry said. Then to the amusement of the bartender, waitress, Terry Ann, who had just walked in from the ladies' room, and the old barfly who scooted over five stools for a closer look, we traded pants. Luckily Jerry's were black.

"Hey, Terry Ann," Jerry said, removing his shoes and pants. "I hear you farted."

"Yeah. I farted," Terry Ann said. "Shouldn't have stopped at Taco Bell before the wedding for a quick bite. Big mistake. Next to John blowing out his bloody nose plugs onto some lady, it was the highlight of the ceremony."

"I almost wish I'd been there," Jerry said.

I removed my pants and underwear simultaneously because the undies really were securely stapled to the pants, then slipped into Jerry's pants. Jerry, who is porkier than me, tore out the shorts from the sprung-zipper pants before squeezing into them, hopping up and down to get them up. The staples gave way and the zipper gapped back open.

"Great," he said, looking down at his exposed lime green underwear. The bar fly started slowly applauding.

"No charge for the floor show," he told her.

"Some show," she sniffed. "I want a refund."

"Elliot, this is no good," Jerry said.

"What do you mean?"

"Now I have the same problem you had. I can't walk around like this at the reception. I'll be inundated with date requests."

"In your dreams," Terry Ann said.

"You can have my cummerbund, Studley," I said.

"You're always so thoughtful, Elliot."

"Can I buy you a drink?" the barfly asked Jerry.

"No," Jerry said. "Hey, Terry Ann."

"What, Jerry?"

"How about a dance at the reception?"

"I'm going to pass."

"Gas?"

"A little one. Just for you."

"I can stand it," Jerry said.

"See you later, Jerry. Let's go, Terry Ann. Bartender, cash me out. I'm getting married."

The Insides Looked Different

Onie Grosshans

The day began with the best of intentions: one friend agreeing to help another friend get through a busy day. Kay and Ellie were recently retired colleagues, comfortable in their decades-long friendship, which began when both had unlined faces, glossy hair, and limber bodies. Now days with deepening smile lines, graying hair, and morning stiffness they easily adjusted to a more relaxed schedule, meeting frequently for Sunday breakfasts at a café near Ellie's home or enjoying summer afternoons talking in either Kay or Ellie's flower-filled backyard while their cats kept watch from under nearby bushes. But truth be told, what they really liked were weekend stays in Wendover, Nevada, a 90-minute drive west of Salt Lake City on I-80, where they spent their time playing the slots. Each had a maximum limit she would spend, but usually both women won enough money on their favorite slot machines to keep playing most of the day, taking breaks for lunch and dinner.

Another gambling trip was planned for the weekend, but Kay wanted to fill her yard waste container for the Monday morning trash pickup before leaving town. She also needed an oil change for her Mazda at Jiffy Lube, as well as having her tires rotated at the Goodyear Tire Store. Thinking through the time needed to trim, weed, and mow, and knowing she didn't want to be rushed in her meticulous lawn care, she phoned Ellie. "Could you take my Mazda for its oil change and tire rotation this morning?"

A transplanted Virginian, Ellie preferred the company of her two cats and the quiet of her own backyard to navigating the busy streets of Salt Lake City, but she agreed to help her friend, a "can do anything" native of Wyoming. It should take less than two hours to do both tasks, Ellie thought, and a good way to repay Kay for repairing her sprinkler system leak earlier this summer.

Ellie parked her faded blue 1979 Corolla station wagon in front of Kay's house, locked the door, and gave the taillight a loving pat as she walked by, thinking they don't make cars like they used to. With a book tucked under one arm, a ball cap covering her gray-flecked curly hair, Ellie, in her increasingly tilted walk, ambled up the driveway in her tennis shoes, blue jeans, and long-sleeved denim shirt with cuffs rolled to her elbows over a T-shirt.

Kay met Ellie at the back door, with the key to the Mazda and an American Express credit card to pay for the oil change. Free tire rotation was part of the deal when Kay bought the tires at Goodyear last spring. With a tinge of apprehension Kay watched as Ellie, moving at a snail's pace, or as some friends would say, "moving at Ellie pace," backed the Mazda out of the long driveway. Ellie had driven Kay's car several times, always commenting on the confusing dashboard, strange steering wheel that could move up or down, and a rearview mirror Ellie thought distorting. Ellie did like the electric windows, but noted, "They'd be expensive to fix if something went wrong."

With a sigh of relief Kay watched the Mazda disappear around the corner, then rolled out the trash can, the lawn mower, and trimmer and started to work. She estimated it would take most of the morning to get everything done the way she wanted it, so Kay was thankful Ellie gave up her quiet morning to help her out.

Two cars were ahead of Ellie when she arrived at Jiffy Lube near her home, so she pulled in line and waited for the attendant with the clipboard to take the necessary information. When asked how long it would take, the young man with a scratchy beard said "about 45 minutes." Ellie left the keys in the car, grabbed her book, and headed for the waiting room but, hearing children yelling, did an abrupt U-turn. Her house was five blocks away and she much preferred reading in the cool shade of her quiet backyard porch than the small waiting area with screaming kids and a loud TV. Ellie's southern drawl still strong after years of living in the north, she told the attendant, "I'll just wander on home and come back in a bit if you don't mind."

About 45 minutes later, Ellie ambled into the now quiet waiting area. "Good timing," said the attendant, "your car is ready to go." Ellie handed over Kay's credit card, not bothering to explain she wasn't Kay, and signed Kay's name.

The attendant gave Ellie a receipt, handed over the keys, and, pointing in the direction of the side of the store, said, "Your car is parked over there."

Settling into the driver's seat, Ellie said to herself, "Why do they make these dashboards so confusing?" Carefully backing up and then merging into heavy morning traffic, Ellie headed to the Goodyear Tire Store, about 20 minutes away. Once again, a lineup of cars waited for service, so Ellie parked in front of the store, grabbed her book, and walked inside to the counter where a young man, with "Bill" emblazoned on his work shirt, sat behind a computer.

"I need to have the tires rotated on that car," Ellie said as she pointed to Kay's car through the plate glass window.

The young man took the car key, saying, "I need to check the mileage," and walked outside carrying a notepad. After a few minutes Bill returned, punched data into the computer, had a quizzical look, punched some more keys, but still look mystified.

"What's the problem, Bill?" asked Ellie.

"I can't find your car in the system," he said. "Are you sure you bought those tires at Goodyear?"

Ellie leaned across the counter, looked the young man in the eyes, and in a polite but firm voice said, "Bill, my friend bought *those* tires at *this* store last April. Your recordkeeping is the problem!"

"But the car isn't in our records," the young man said.

"I'm telling you my friend bought those tires here because I was with her when she did it, and she needs them rotated today."

Assessing the determined woman in the baseball cap across the counter from him, the young man nodded in agreement.

"Take a seat and I'll let you know when your car is ready."

"Thank you," Ellie said as she headed toward a corner seat in the quiet waiting area and opened her book. About 30 minutes later Bill stood in the doorway and said, "Your Camry is ready."

"I don't have a Camry," Ellie said. "I have a Mazda."

"You drove a Camry here."

"No, I drove here in a Mazda," said Ellie in the stern professorial voice she once used in her classrooms.

"I'm sorry, lady, but the tires we just rotated for you are located on that Camry parked over there."

That's when it dawned on Ellie what happened.

She had driven away in the wrong car at Jiffy Lube. She thanked the exasperated young man, took the Camry key, and walked quickly to somebody else's car whose tires had just been rotated and headed back to Jiffy Lube.

While stopped at a traffic light, Ellie noticed she was behind a police car. When the light turned green the patrol car headed through the intersection, followed by Ellie. The two cars continued in the same direction, taking the same turns. Ellie could see the Jiffy Lube store so she turned on her right blinker and noticed the patrol car also blinked its intention to turn right.

A frantic Jiffy Lube attendant ran to the police car, closely followed by a frantic middle-aged woman, and both converged on the officer before he could open his car door. No one noticed Ellie pulling in behind the patrol car. Ellie got out of the Camry, approached the trio, and calmly said, "There's been a mistake."

The stunned trio, with jaws gaping, stared at Ellie. It took several minutes to sort out the confusion. With calm restored, the Jiffy

Lube guy, relieved to be off the hook for giving a customer the wrong car key, the Camry owner, thankful to have her car returned undamaged *and* with the extra benefit of a tire rotation, meant nobody wanted to press charges against anyone, but they all wondered why Ellie didn't immediately recognize she was driving the wrong car. "Well," drawled Ellie, "it seemed to be the same color, but I did think there was something a bit different with the insides."

The Camry owner, laughing, said, "My husband will never believe me when I tell him what happened." The policeman said, "This is a new one for me," and the relieved Jiffy Lube guy disappeared into the store returning with the key to the Mazda, saying to Ellie, "I'll take you to your car."

Sitting in the Mazda, Ellie realized she still needed to get Kay's tires rotated for the Wendover trip, so she again carefully backed up, cussing "no one can see out of these mirrors," and merged the Mazda into noon day traffic, headed to the Goodyear Tire Store. Parking behind a car lined up at one of the bays, Ellie walked in the store, and seeing Bill, the same young man she had intimidated, frustrated, and exasperated earlier in the day, pointed out the window saying, "*This* is the car whose tires you were supposed to rotate."

This time the computer did find Kay's car, and Bill, trying not to laugh as he looked at Ellie, said, "We'll take care of it."

With her mowing, clipping, trimming, and weeding finished some time ago, Kay wondered what was keeping Ellie. Going inside her house to fix herself a peanut butter sandwich, Kay heard the beeping of her answering machine. Pressing the button Kay listened to several messages from Jiffy Lube wanting her to call the store immediately. I wonder what happened, she thought, but just then she saw her Mazda edging its way toward the garage, so Kay pressed the Save button and headed to the back door.

"Thanks, Ellie," Kay said. "Can I fix you a sandwich?"

Ellie shook her head with a definite no, handed Kay the car key, credit card, and receipts, and, with her book tucked under her arm, strolled down the driveway toward her trusty Corolla, saying, "It's late. I gotta get home. See you in the morning."

"By the way, Ellie," Kay called after her, "why does Jiffy Lube want me to call them?"

Trouble at the Supermarket

Albert Howard Carter, III

Ah, vacation at the beach! Mellow, lazy, slow. Sarah and I take long walks by the surf, have meals whenever we want. Reading, naps, drinks before dinner. We've been reading detective and spy fiction. I'm reading Clancy and Ludlum. She's reading Grafton and Sayers. Apparently, we enjoy—amidst all this indolence and ease—tantalizing if hypothetical dangers that are cleverly and speedily solved.

Unfortunately, our time is almost over: just a few more days and back home we go.

"Ted, we're all out of fruit. Let's get some," Sarah says.

"Gosh, we're only here for three or four more days."

"I know, but I like having it, and the store's not far."

"It's not a very nice store."

"No, but they sure as heck have fruit."

"It's not an A&P, so they can't possibly have the girl with breasts like two scoops of vanilla ice cream."

"What are you babbling about?"

"That's from a John Updike story, certainly the best line."

"Oh, you MEN!"

"Yep, that's us."

So, we drive over there and pick out some fruit that's ready to eat. I drift down the wine aisle, just for fun, and see a large cooler. Aha, there's a bottle of champagne inside! In a festive mood, I open the door and take out the chilled bottle.

The check-out girl has a tag reading "Lou Ann." She's a slender brunette with purple streaks in her hair.

"You folks on vacation," she says—hard to tell whether it's a question or a statement.

"Yes," we say as Lou Ann rings up the fruit and champagne.

"So's just about everybody that comes here," she says, putting everything in a plastic bag. (At home, we have cloth bags to help the environment.) I don't like how the champagne bottle will chill the fruit and maybe even bruise it, so I pull it out and carry it in my hand.

"Wait a sec," Sarah says. "I might need something else." She goes back carrying the bag. I stand there a moment, then walk over to a magazine rack well off to the side. To my surprise, they stock *National Geographic*. Maybe it'll have an article on somewhere we've traveled or where Jason Bourne has been on his adventures. I stick the bottle under my arm so I can flip through the latest issue. A security guard approaches me.

"Hey, mister." He points to my bottle. "You pay for that?" He's a big guy in a fancy uniform. He has a pistol on his hip.

"Sure thing. Just went through Lou Ann's register. You can ask her."

"I need to see your sales slip."

"Well, if you can wait just a moment, my wife's got it in the bag, and she went back for something."

"I need to see your sales slip," he repeats.

This guy is starting to annoy me.

"Sure, no problem. I'll locate my wife."

"I need it *now*, because no slip, no merchandise," he says, holding out his hand for my bottle. "Merchandise" sounds like a big word for him.

Just my luck on a lovely day.

"Hey, now, hang on a moment," I say, drawing the bottle back. "I can have a slip for you very, very soon."

Instead, he grabs for the bottle, pushing me in the process. As I pull back, some long-ago lessons in martial arts guide my reflexes.

"Watch it," I say, going into a crouch and dropping the *National Geographic*.

"*You* watch it," he says, lunging hard for my bottle with both hands.

I slip to the side and automatically hit him in the front of his neck with the side of my free hand, hard. He falls to his knees, choking. One hand reaches for his pistol.

Is this creep going to shoot me?

I hit him on the head with my bottle, as hard as I can. The bottle doesn't break, and he falls to the side, out cold.

I spin around, my hands raised, ready for any other attacker. My pulse hammers in my ears.

Well, he started it, flashes through my mind, like for any eight-year-old.

I get hold of myself. We can straighten this out.

First, this guy needs help. I pull out my cell phone and enter 911 as I walk back to the registers.

I hear two rings, then, "This is 911. What is your emergency?"

"There's a guy passed out in the supermarket."

"OK, which one? What address, sir?"

I reach Lou Ann's register. She doesn't know what's happened.

"Lou Ann, what mall is this?"

"Ocean Mall."

"Ocean Mall," I tell the dispatcher.

"Right. We're on the way. ETA four minutes."

I walk over to the manager's office. It's clearly marked and has opaque windows, probably one-way glass. I want to get this all clear.

I set my champagne to the side and knock on the door, which immediately flies open. A shotgun sticks out right into my face, a small man on the other end of it.

"You no move!" he screeches. The mouth of the weapon looks huge. I reflexively duck and sweep my arm up and away, knocking the barrel high. The gun discharges with a terrific BOOM close to my ear. Lou Ann screams.

My God, everyone's crazy here!

I grasp the barrel and spin my body away, pulling the little man out of his office and twisting the weapon from his grasp. He stumbles and falls. He kneels on the floor, hands outstretched.

"No shoot! No shoot! Police coming," he cries in a high, frantic voice. A few other shoppers have dodged down the aisles. Lou Ann is hiding behind her counter.

Sarah sticks her head out from an aisle.

"Ted! You OK?" she yells.

"Yes, but it's all crazy!" I yell back. My ears ring from the gunshot.

"Let's get out of here!" Her eyes are flashing.

"Right."

I try to take stock, but all I can think of is the smoking shotgun in my hands. I work the pump, spewing red shells onto the floor until it's empty. I pull a handkerchief from my pocket and wipe it down. I set it on the floor and kick it under the lined-up shopping carts. Sarah arrives; she picks up the shells and puts them in our bag. I'm sure as hell not leaving without my champagne, so I grab that and put it in the bag as well. The little man has run away. He must have called the cops already. The fallen guard doesn't move.

We rush for the door.

"Wait," I say, my hand on her arm. "Let's take it slow and easy."

"Slow . . . and . . . easy," she gasps out.

We walk deliberately to our rental car and load our purchases in the back seat, just like this was a regular shopping trip. I hear a siren approaching. We get in and I slowly drive to a side exit, while a police car screeches to a halt at the front of the store, lights flashing, doors flying open.

"My God, what the hell . . . happened?" Sarah asks. I try to talk, but can't, so I just wave my hand. My heart is still racing, and my blood pressure must be on the ceiling. My ears ring. My breathing is fast, too fast.

"Don't know . . . if I can talk . . . heart's banging away. Better pull . . . o . . . ver."

"You bet, the sooner . . . the better!"

I pull into a gas station and park over to the side.

I take several deep, slow breaths.

"Well . . . this big rent-a-cop . . . thought I stole the . . . champagne. He pushed me around. And . . . um, I'm sorry to say . . . well, the truth of it is . . . that I hit him and . . . knocked him out cold."

"You WHAT?"

"Crazy, I know. But he started it."

"Oh, you MEN!"

"Well, he did! And . . . and we can't change that now."

"Knocked him out? How ever?"

"With the champagne bottle."

"Oh no! That's terrible. Just terrible. The wine will be all fizzy!"

"I fear it will."

"Oh dear, oh dear . . . oh dear!"

"Well, do you think we should have stayed and explained everything to the police?"

"Well, I don't know. It's all so . . . absurd."

"Definitely, most definitely. Let's see. They'll have Lou Ann's word . . . and the register tape . . . proving that we bought the champagne."

"Right. And you paid cash, so no credit card trail."

"Ah yes. Good. And if the security cameras caught my scuffle with the guard, it will be clear that he pushed me."

"Yes. Would any of your conversation be on it?"

"I don't think so, but that would be conclusive if it were."

"And what about the manager?"

"Well, that's assault with a deadly weapon."

"I guess so, but he'd argue self-defense, in case you took the guard's pistol."

"True, but I clearly didn't."

"And you called 911. Surely that shows, well, good faith."

"Damn right it does. Boatloads of good faith!"

There's an awkward pause.

"Gosh, Ted. What are we going to do? Should we go back?"

"I don't know, but, quite frankly, I don't want to go back there ever again."

Sarah blows out a large breath. "Well, all I know is that I heard a loud gunshot, I ran down the aisle to make sure you were OK, and there you were . . . holding a smoking gun, a guy's on the floor begging for mercy, and the security man is laid out over on the side."

"Didn't look good, did it?"

"No, not at all, not in the very least."

"Well, I don't have a history of that sort of thing, now do I?"

Sarah starts to laugh. "No, you don't, that's for sure, but you've surprised me before, and you know what they say about old dogs," she wheezes out. I start to laugh too, and pretty soon we're guffawing like hyenas and slapping the dashboard between outbursts. Upon one hit, I find that my hand is sore where I slugged the guard. I pull the champagne from the back seat and arrange the bottle along my thigh so I can chill my hand on it as we drive back to our place.

Somehow the mood for our vacation has changed, so we decide to go home the next day. Besides, I'm worried about the guard. I'm not as strong as I was in college decades ago, but there's a chance that I broke his neck . . . killed him . . . then left the scene!

This worries me a lot, so we start to scan TV stations, luckily finding a 24-hour channel for local news.

A good-looking young man in a suit smiles and says, "The Ocean Mall supermarket was robbed early this afternoon by an elderly man, but, apparently, all he took was a bottle of champagne."

"What?!" Sarah and I exclaim.

His news-reading partner, a knockout blonde, shakes her curls and adds, "Those *crazy* tourists—especially this time of year!"

"That's right, Tiffany, it was a daring daylight robbery, for just one bottle of booze, which he then used to *attack* the security guard!"

"Oh, that's just great, Frank," Tiffany chirps, "using the stolen goods as a *weapon*!"

"No!" I burst out.

Frank smiles, showing expensive teeth, and continues, "And that's not all, because then the elderly man stormed the manager's office, again with his bottle, and we have an interview with the manager."

The screen shows the manager, now wearing a tie, and speaking calmly: "Yes, he attack my office with the bottle, but I was able to stop him with my . . . um . . . pistol . . . which he stole also."

"Ha," I yell. "A shotgun would be illegal there!"

"Shhhhhhh," Sarah hisses.

Frank smiles again, flashing teeth, "Luckily a *responsible* shopper was able to call 911 and get the police and paramedics there quickly!"

Tiffany beams. "At least there are still some *sane* people at the beach!"

"Me, you idiots!" I yell. "It was ME who called!"

Mr. Teeth continues, "After treatment by paramedics, the guard refused further help and went back to work!"

"So," Tiffany gushes, "all's well that ends well, except for the *theft of a bottle of champagne*!"

"I guess so," Teeth concludes. "The police say they are investigating but have no leads."

I yell at the TV, "I PAID for it, dammit!"

Sarah shouts. "And we have the sales slip!"

Blondie smiles, showing more wonderful teeth. "And now to the weather. Another gorgeous day in paradise, eh, Wally?"

I punch the remote to shut off the TV.

"Bastards! All of them," I declare. "Well, thank God the guard's OK."

"Thank God," Sarah affirms. "Actually, I was scared about that."

"Yeah, me too."

We look each other in the eyes for moment, then smile.

"Clearly, this calls for champagne," I say, rubbing my hand, a little sore, but not broken.

"Exactly," she says.

I get two glasses, hoping the champagne won't explode all over our kitchenette. After all, it's had a rough day and has been accused, publicly, on television, of participation in felonious acts.

I ease out the cork. There's a nice pop and some emerging effervescence, but I have the glasses right there and pour intermittently and carefully. "Those clowns, they spun it all wrong." I mutter.

"A pack of lies to be sure, but, when you think about it, pretty clever . . . in its own way."

"In a way, but those hotshot TV people sure didn't show a picture of the shotgun blast on the ceiling, now did they?"

"No, and I wonder what insurance will say about that."

"Ha, ha, ha," I laugh. "If, that is, that ever gets reported."

"Yeah, *if*."

We clink our glasses together, smile at each other, and drink.

She looks at her champagne. "So, is this now considered contraband?"

"According to them, yeah. But, to tell the truth, you're the only thief here."

"Whatever do you mean?"

"You took the manager's shotgun shells, even the spent one."

"Ha," she says. "You're right. I'm a thief!"

"Yeah, and that makes me an accomplice."

"Darn tootin'."

We drink to that.

But you know what's the absolutely worst thing?" I say.

"What?"

"Those TV people called me 'elderly'!"

"Oh, now *that* is a crime," Sarah says. "It really is."

Fistfight with a Deer

Becky Jensen

My older sister, Christy, stood over me as I packed my suitcase, holding her baby on her hip. "You won't need that," she said, removing the curling iron. "Or that," she said, pointing to the can of hairspray, eyeballing my perfectly feathered hair. She had invited me to stay at a remote cabin in western Colorado where she lived with her husband. I had no idea what I was in for.

It was the summer of 1983. I was a city kid, awkward and gangly, about to turn 13. *Return of the Jedi* was breaking box office records, "Every Breath You Take" ruled the radio, and Ronald Reagan was in the White House. The popular kids my age wore Izod polo shirts with popped collars. Had cable television with MTV. They hung out in preppy packs drinking Orange Julius shakes at the mall and swam at private neighborhood pools. How I longed to be one of them.

Whatever cabin life would be like, spending a few weeks with my married sister had to be better than hearing about the other kids having fun while I babysat, mowed lawns, and weeded the garden all summer. I begged my parents to let me go.

Christy threw my suitcase in the trunk and buckled my nephew in his car seat. After tuning the radio to a country station, we drove west—far from the urban Front Range of Colorado, deep into sparsely populated Moffat County, toward a remote region known as Brown's Park.

The area had a reputation as outlaw country.

During its Wild West heyday in the late 1800s, Brown's Park had been crawling with cattle rustlers and train robbers, including Butch Cassidy and the Sundance Kid, and their band the Wild Bunch.

The legendary Outlaw Trail—a series of hideaways that stretched from Montana to Mexico—ran through Brown's Park. Bandits like the Wild Bunch were regulars on this secret renegade network and used the area's unforgiving terrain and labyrinth of canyons to evade capture.

Nearly a century later, my brother-in-law, Tom, rode that same range on horseback. His job was to check cow camps and bail hay on a cattle ranch that had been in his family for generations. He and Christy and the baby lived in an original homestead cabin without electricity or running water, its only modern convenience a propane-powered fridge and freezer. The spread lay east of the Utah border, and south of the Wyoming line, near the old Outlaw Trail.

My sister couldn't say if the ranch had been a hidey hole for bandits and bank robbers. But she *had* unwittingly named her baby after a notorious uncle on my brother-in-law's side of the family. The namesake relative, according to family lore, had shot and killed his own brother at the supper table one night in the 1930s.

By comparison, my sister and I had such a vanilla family history. Our people were simple farmers from Sweden and Denmark who settled in Iowa and eventually migrated into towns. As a city girl, I felt far removed from our farming roots and great-grandparents who braved the voyage to America by boat. Light years away from our fierce Viking ancestors who struck fear and swords into the hearts of those they conquered.

Christy was 16 years older than me, and I idolized the beautiful sister I rarely saw and hardly knew. When I was little, she would patiently sit on the floor of our cramped apartment and let me brush the long hair that cascaded down her back like amber honey. My stomach fluttered before each of her visits, anticipating the warmth of my sister's velvet-smooth voice, her silken hair between my fingers, that movie-star smile.

Christy shared our dad's romantic love of the American Wild West. So it was no surprise when she fell for a lanky cowboy with a charming drawl, and soon married into a family of real-deal Colorado ranchers.

By the time Christy, the baby, and I arrived at the cabin in Brown's Park, it was past bedtime and we were bone tired. Tom greeted us at the low door to the cabin, a warm glow spilling from the small kitchen into the summer night. He was dressed in mud-caked cowboy boots, Wrangler jeans, and a plaid western shirt with pearl snaps. His hair lay smashed flat where his cowboy hat had pressed against his scalp all day.

"Howdy! C'mon in," he called out.

"Shh, don't wake the baby," Christy hushed before giving Tom a quick kiss.

The cabin's interior was a time capsule. A fire crackled in the kitchen's antique cast iron stove, the log walls were chinked thick with mortar, and worn Naugahyde furniture with wagon-wheel arm rests filled the living room.

I picked up a small jar from a table and nearly dropped it on the hardwood floor. An enormous beetle filled the glass, its sharp mandible pincers reaching for the metal lid.

"Isn't that neat?" Christy whispered, swaying back and forth with the sleeping baby. "I caught it in that room right over there."

She pointed to a dark bedroom.

"Where . . . am I sleeping?" I managed to choke out.

"In that room, right over there," she repeated, pointing to the same bedroom.

I tried to convince my sister I'd be fine sleeping on the couch, that I *loved* sleeping on the couch, but she just walked me over to the "beetle room" I would share with my nephew. After changing his diaper, she nursed the baby and laid him down in his crib.

"Can I use the bathroom?" I asked, shifting from foot to foot.

"You mean the outhouse," my sister corrected. She grabbed a kerosene lantern and led me outside down a dirt path to a phonebooth-sized shack. Christy handed me the lantern, opened the creaking slab door, and waved me into the dark privy. The stench of ammonia stung my eyes and nose as I latched the hook behind me. Someone had bolted an indoor toilet seat over a gaping hole on a boxy wooden platform. I hung the lantern on a hook, dropped my drawers, and situated myself on the primitive toilet.

"You might not want to sit down," she called through the door, making me jump. "The black widows like to nest under the seat."

I bolted from the outhouse, hitching up my pants as I sped down the path. My sister tried hard to hide a grin.

Back inside the cabin, I said goodnight and closed the bedroom door behind me. I climbed under the covers without brushing my teeth. It was pitch black in the room, and I was too embarrassed to tell my sister that I was afraid of the dark. And that beetle. And those poisonous spiders in the outhouse. Mice began to scurry overhead in the attic, and I cried myself to sleep.

By morning, my quilt was covered in mystery grit and tiny bits of wood. I looked above me, and figured the debris must have dropped from the crude log ceiling. Each time I moved, more bits of bark and dirt fell from my hair. I shook my head over the quilt.

My nephew laughed from his crib, standing in his striped jammies, gripping the slats with his chubby fists like a jailbird. I scooped him up.

"Oh, you think that's funny?" I said to the baby, shaking my hair again. He giggled harder.

We walked into the kitchen where my sister sipped a cup of coffee by the wood stove. After handing off the baby, I headed outside to the dreaded privy and stopped short, frozen on the path.

"Uh, Christy?" I called nervously. "Can you come out here, please?"

The ranch dogs were acting peculiar, circling a scruffy-looking mule deer in the yard. I turned my head just enough to see my sister approaching from behind, her face full of worry. I pointed at the cornered wild animal with its donkey-like ears and lopsided antlers—one horn a six-inch stump covered in velvet, the other barely a nub.

"Oh, that's just Cookie," she said in relief. "He's our pet deer."

As I watched more closely, I realized the young buck was playing with the dogs, as if establishing his place in the pack. The yearling ate dog chow from a bowl. And when the ranch dogs barked, the deer joined them, making a bizarre nasal sound.

"*Joey, joey*," Cookie bleated, aiming his horn at an overly rambunctious dog.

"He's so tame, we have to tie orange to his antlers during hunting season so he doesn't get shot," Christy said.

My brother-in-law walked past us toward the house. He'd been up for hours.

"I'd shoot and butcher it m'self," he muttered, clearing a wad of wet chewing tobacco from his lower lip with the sweep of a finger. "But I think it's got the mange."

I looked at Tom in horror.

My sister told me how Cookie had earned his name and came to live on the ranch the previous summer. The orphaned fawn walked through an open door and into her father-in-law's house one afternoon. Tom's dad found the young animal sprawled on his waterbed, asleep, after having devoured an entire plate of fresh-baked cookies. Eventually, the fawn imprinted on the ranch dogs, learned to eat kibble, and thought he was part of the pack.

"How cool to have a pet deer," I said in awe, reaching my fingers toward Cookie to touch his dull, patchy coat. In an instant, the animal bolted away. A truck had pulled into the ranch, and the young deer, with his rowdy pack of dogs, chased after it.

Over the next few weeks, I grew to love the rugged landscape at our remote post on the Outlaw Trail. I helped my brother-in-law hook hay bales onto a sled as he drove the tractor around the meadow. Slogged barefoot through the mud to catch frogs. Explored washouts in search of arrowheads. I was too busy having fun to think about Izod shirts. The mall. MTV.

I hardly bathed, and ate supper with dirt under my fingernails. The mice scurried at night, and I slept soundly as soft bits of ceiling rained down on my head. I had no idea what my hair looked like, and didn't care. There was an ease to cabin living, a freedom in acting unladylike, and I was beginning to appreciate this simpler lifestyle and grittier version of myself.

Everyday chores were more like adventures than simple mind-numbing tasks. After fetching water from the pump one day, my sister showed me how to wash clothes using a gas-powered ringer washing machine she kept in the yard. To start it up, Christy yanked on a cord like a lawn mower. It took three pulls before it belched exhaust and came to life. After sudsing and rinsing the clothes, my sister fed items through the wringer to squeeze out excess water, and I caught them on the other side. Fabric emerged from between the two rollers, long and flat, like wide lasagna noodles from a pasta machine.

As Christy hung clean cloth diapers on the line to dry, I walked over to a gentle horse I had ridden the day before. He was tied to the horse trailer, no saddle in sight. The old version of Becky, the careful and good girl so eager to please, would have helped her sister hang laundry. Would have asked permission to ride the gelding again. But the new Wild West version of me, the outlaw "Becky the Kid," was plotting how to jump onto the horse bareback to escape an imaginary posse.

"Easy," I said softly, untying the animal and leading him over to a large boulder. "Easy, fella."

The horse's ears pricked up—one pointed forward, and the other turned sideways toward me—as I climbed on top of the rock. His skin rippled, shaking off biting flies under the midday sun.

With the lead rope in one hand, I blew out a long breath and leapt from the boulder toward the horse's broad back. As I sailed through the air, the gelding took a single step away from me, and I landed in a cloud of dust on the hard ground. I brushed off my pants, climbed onto the same rock, and jumped toward the horse's back a second time. Without a glance in my direction, the animal sidestepped me again.

By then, Christy had made her way over from the clothesline. I stood up and rubbed my sore backside, trying to read my sister's face, worried that I was in trouble. She just smiled and held the halter so I could climb onto the rock again. I leapt a third time and landed on the horse's warm back. The animal smelled of sweet hay, the dry corral, the sharp tang of his sweat. Grabbing a handful of mane, I walked the horse around the outbuildings, riding bareback for the first time, my knees gripped around his belly. The sun kissed my beaming cheeks.

In the days following that bareback ride, I walked with a little more swagger. Brown's Park was teaching me I could take risks and was tougher than I thought. One afternoon, Tom took me out in the battered pickup, and we bounced along old ranch roads through a sea of sagebrush and greasewood. He spotted a herd of pronghorn antelope, stopped to pull his rifle off the gun rack, and poached a buck.

"Ever had antelope steak?" He winked, heaving the carcass into the bed of the truck. Before Brown's Park, I'd been a kid who always followed the rules. Being Tom's accomplice thrilled me to the core.

Although I'd adapted to the rough-and-ready way of life on the ranch, part of me felt like a big phony. I missed sleeping in a bed without having to check for critters under the covers. I longed for hot showers, hair conditioner, and a sparkling-clean toilet located inside the house. The thoughts made me feel soft, like a pampered city slicker unable to cut it in the cowboy world. As if I was betraying my newfound toughness.

To prove I wasn't chicken, I dared myself to pull off one final deed before heading back home.

Cookie browsed in the side yard, away from his pack of dogs. For weeks I had vowed to pet the scruffy orphan. Mange or no mange, this was my last chance. I tiptoed toward the small deer with an outstretched hand.

"Hey, Cookie," I spoke softly. "I won't hurt ya."

Cookie stopped nibbling a shrub, lifted his head, and stared into my eyes.

I stepped closer to the yearling.

He stamped the ground.

I reached an open palm toward his neck.

He lowered his big ears.

"*Joey!*" Cookie bleated in warning.

I took another step forward.

He reared up on his hind legs. "*Joey! Joey!*"

Before I knew it, the scrawny deer lunged at me, bringing his front hooves down on my collar bones. He barely missed my face. It took a few seconds to register that my sister's mongrel pet deer was attacking me. And my immediate response, for better or worse, was to put up a fight.

I grabbed Cookie's forelegs and threw him to the ground. He reared up again, his sharp hooves crashing down on my shoulders, trying to push me off balance. We wrestled. I grabbed Cookie by his one weird antler and threw him down again.

Before I knew it, my brother-in-law had stepped in front of the deer to put an end to our brawl.

"Gaw-dammit, Cookie!" Tom hollered.

The deer tried to charge me again.

My brother-in-law was done talking.

Like a classic bar fight in a western movie, Tom cocked back his elbow and punched the animal square in the jaw. Cookie reeled and fell to the dirt, then staggered to his feet, dazed and wobbly. Then the deer did something so humanlike, the visual has stuck with me for more than 40 years—Cookie slowly moved his bottom jaw up and down, and side to side, testing it out after the punch.

The young buck finally shook his head and bounded off into the brush, as if getting coldcocked by a steel-fisted cowboy wasn't a big deal. And my brother-in-law, completely unfazed, moseyed back to the cabin.

"What just happened?" I asked the empty sky as my body shook with adrenaline.

To calm my breathing, I walked a few laps around the cabin and down the driveway, trying to make sense of it all. *Pets are supposed to behave*, I told myself. *They're supposed to be tame.*

A few days after the fight with Cookie, it was time for me to go home. School would start soon. Christy drove me to the bus station in the town of Craig, and handed me a cold, heavy package about the size of a football. It was a frozen pronghorn rump roast, hard as a rock, wrapped in layers of butcher paper.

"Give this to Dad, okay?" she said, handing over the contraband. "And maybe don't tell him exactly how we got it."

I boarded the Greyhound and found a seat by the window. Christy waved from the sidewalk as the bus pulled away. I waved back, a 13-year-old girl riding a bus more than 200 miles home. Alone. I smiled at my sister, replaying memories and lessons learned from Brown's Park to bolster my courage.

Christy had chosen the bold cowboy lifestyle. During my visit, she gave me the freedom to try new things without telling me no, without reminding me to be careful. My sister encouraged me to jump, fall in the dirt, and get back on that horse. She showed me I didn't have to follow a tame, predictable path as a female.

My brother-in-law had watched out for me, but hadn't coddled me. That wouldn't have helped me out there. He never apologized for bending the rules or the rough way things were often done on the ranch. Tom, in his unconventional manner, taught me to roll with the punches and not care so much about what others think.

I thought of my tussle with Cookie. Just because an animal was *called* a pet, I realized, didn't mean it was tame. That deer was a wild creature at heart. And although I was a city girl trying to fit in with the pack of popular kids, it didn't mean I was completely tame. Turns out I had some wild instincts, too. Spending time on the ranch didn't mean

I'd lost the softer side of me or my respect for the law. It didn't mean that city living was all bad, and country living was all good, or vice versa. We are never all tame or all wild, all bad or all good, all rule-follower or all outlaw. We're almost always a mix, riding in and out of the canyon shadows as we make our choices throughout life.

As I rode off into the sunset on my Greyhound with a stolen antelope roast thawing in my lap, it felt like I'd been busted out of jail and was on the run. Brown's Park had unlocked a wild, free-spirited side of me that I never knew existed before.

I had thrived in the land of outlaw in-laws. Rode a horse bareback. Survived a fistfight with a deer.

The dust of the Outlaw Trail had me thirsting for more. Like maybe a sweet, ice-cold Orange Julius at the mall. When I got back to town, I'd swagger into that food court, slam my hard-earned babysitting money down on the counter, and order myself a tall one. On my own.

I was Becky the Kid, willing to take a leap.

Bold. Unapologetic.

Ready to grab life by the horns. Or, at the very least, by one weird antler.

Contributors

Steve Holland is a retired teacher who taught high school English for 31 years in southeastern Indiana.

Allan M. Heller has published dozens of poems, short stories, and seven nonfiction books. In February 2014 he was appointed poet laureate of Hatboro, Pennsylvania. In addition to being a writer, Heller has tutored students in GED and SAT test preparation, as well as ESL. He is a 1988 graduate of Indiana University of Pennsylvania.

Shauna Hicks is totally tickled to be in this TulipTree issue. Her background is Broadway, where she specialized in making leading men look tall. Most notably David Cassidy and Ralph Macchio. Shauna has sung in symphony halls and concert venues all over the world, but her favorite, hands down, was singing Judy Garland songs in Liza Minelli's living room. Shauna lives in New York City with her husband, son, and two cats.

David Margolis is a retired gastroenterologist living in St. Louis, MO. His stories have appeared in the *Canadian Medical Association Journal*, *JAMA: Internal Medicine*, *Missouri Medicine*, *HumorPress.com*, and the *Baby Boomers Plus 2021* anthology. He's published three books of short stories, *Looking Behind*, *Meltdown*, and *Tales of Unkosher Souls*. *Tales* was selected by Kirkus Reviews as a Best Indie Book of 2021. Previously, he published three novels, *The Myth of Dr. Kugelman*, *The Plumber's Wrench*, and *The Misadventures of Buddy Jones*, which won an eLit award for humor and was presented at the Jewish Book Festival of St. Louis. David has recently completed two full-length comedic plays, *Two Goats and a Dog* and *The Dybbuk of Brooklyn*, as well as several short plays. His plays have been read at the University of Missouri Playwrights Workshop and at First Run Theater in St. Louis.

Lyss Buchthal (they/them) is a US-based writer whose work centers queer Americana, primarily themes on identity, perception, and power. Lyss's writing appears or is forthcoming in *The Orange & Bee, Rat Bag Literary, foofaraw, Pipeline Artists,* and *Neon Dystopia*.

Eva Kappel is a classical historian with a particular interest in Roman inscriptions and in Greek papyri from ancient Egypt. Born and raised near the river Rhine, she currently works in the conservation of ancient monuments in Munich, Germany. In her free time, she can often be seen roaming across the Bavarian countryside, taking inspiration from its wild and wonderful culture and landscape. This is her first non-academic publication.

Martin Settle is a writer in Charlotte, NC. He has taught English for 32 years, the last 17 of which were at UNC Charlotte. He has published eight books (two memoirs, an art design book, a joke book, and four books of poetry). In addition, he has been awarded the Thomas McDill Award (North Carolina Poetry Society), the Poetry of Courage Award (North Carolina Poetry Society), the Nazim Hikmet Poetry Award, and the Griffin-Farlow Haiku Award, and he has been published in *The New York Times*.

Brad G. Philbrick, RPh, is a pharmacist-turned-writer who blends decades of experience in pharmacy, biomedical sales, and grant writing with a passion for creative nonfiction. After more than 40 years in healthcare, Brad now devotes his work to helping others live safer, healthier, and more intentional lives through insightful writing. He is the founder of Brad G. Philbrick & Company, where he provides grant development, copywriting, and educational content for healthcare and nonprofit organizations. His reflections on science, wellness, and human behavior appear regularly on bradgphilbrick.com and on Medium. "From pills to prose," Brad believes that the art of health lies not just in medicine—but in mindfulness, curiosity, and connection.

Meredith Meyer is a writer and musician who grew up in Oklahoma. After moving around a lot, she ended up in LA, where she got her start as a songwriter. This took her to NY, where she played in multiple bands including Young Unknowns and Easy Dreams, her current music project with partner Brandon White. She loves mysteries, synthesizers, and their two cats. She's currently working on her debut novel, "Along the Stardust Highway," about the hidden nightlife of a rural town.

In addition to her career as an educator, **Dar Thomas** has published short stories in various literary journals, including *Solstice Literary Magazine* and *American Writers Review*. Two of Dar's stories have been awarded Honorable Mention and First Place in the Westmoreland Arts & Heritage Short Story Contest; another story ranked as a finalist in the 47th New Millennium Award for Flash Fiction. Dar lives in Pittsburgh, PA, with her artist husband and their rescue pup, Gaia.

Liz Kelner Pozen is a Boston-based artist and retired psychotherapist. She has shown her work throughout New England, and her paintings are largely figurative and contain psychological content. Although informed by past experiences and memories, like Rorschach blots, they contain multiple meanings and interpretations. Some themes found throughout her work include family dynamics, identity, and memory. In addition to her art career, she has written three books of poetry: *The Heart of the Family*, *Salami*, and *A Scarred Samovar*. She has also written three books for children: *Grandma Can't Hear*, *The What Ifs*, and *Sam and the Number 8*.

Adam Archer ran a large consulting business for over 40 years before turning to writing. He received his BA from Colgate University (surprisingly), MA from Dominican University (slowly), and MFA from Fairfield University (deliberately). He lives in California with his wife of many years. He has three children, three grandchildren, and three great-grandchildren, but he is not as old as he looks. He has written several business monographs, articles, and short books, none of which are particularly interesting, but some of his clients liked them. This is his first personal essay to see print.

K.Z. Steel is a lawyer who dabbles in creative writing. Although this is her first time at the publishing rodeo, she has a long and storied career composing haikus about the Detroit Lions' penchant for stealing defeat from the jaws of victory, roasting friends and colleagues with piping hot limericks, tracking the comings and goings of neighborhood rapscallions, and chronicling her one-sided beef with a mediocre local ice cream shop. Karen lives in New York with her husband, Ryan, their two sons, and their benevolent overlord/cat, Judge.

Richard D. Key was born in Jacksonville, Florida, but grew up in Mississippi. He now lives in southern Alabama, where he works part-time as a pathologist. He has been writing essays and short stories for about 15 years, and his writing has appeared in *Adelaide Literary Magazine*, *American Writers Review*, *Bacopa Literary Review*, *The Birmingham Arts Journal*, *The Broken Plate*, *Carbon Culture Review*, *Crack the Spine*, *Edify Fiction*, *Evening Street Review*, *Forge*, *Hawaii Pacific Review*, *HCE Review*, *October Hill*, *The Penmen Review*, *Storgy*, *Streetlight Magazine*, *THEMA*, and *Tusculum Review*. His author website is richardkeyauthor.com.

Aili Whalen, JD, PhD, is a former ballet dancer, lawyer, and philosophy professor who is now trying her hand at creative writing. For more on Aili see www.artistsmatter.com. She lives in Louisville, KY, with her husband, a chihuahua pug, and a yellow-eared slider (a kind of turtle). "Animal Husbandry" was inspired by a dream she had after traveling abroad and feeling a bit out of touch with the local customs and culture. The fictional location in the story, "Xingoux," is a tongue-in-check reference to "Xingu," Edith Wharton's humorous story by that name.

Geoffrey K. Graves has been published/honored internationally: Cutthroat Barry Lopez Nonfiction Award finalist (US, 2019); Grindstone Literary Anthology winner (UK, 2020); Tobias Wolff Award finalist (US, 2021); Bath Flash Fiction Award shortlist (Ireland, 2021); Periscope Literary 2nd place (UK, 2022); Writers Digest honorable mention (US, 2023, 2025); Witcraft honorable mention (Australia, 2023); Pushcart Nominee honorable mention (US, 2023/24); Disquiet Prize longlist (Portugal, 2024); WestWord Spotlight Story (UK, 2024); Next Generation Short Story Award shortlist/finalist (US, 2025); Little Old Lady Comedy (US, 2025); Awfully Hilarious (Canada, 2025); McClaren Memorial Comedy Festival One-Act Play finalist/winner (US, 2025); and elsewhere. His novella "My Dangerous Romance with the Immortal Randy San Francisco," was a candidate for the Fugere Book Prize (US, 2025). He worked in the Script Department at CBS, Television City, Hollywood, and was CEO/Owner of Graves Advertising. He has directed plays and musicals in Los Angeles and Orange Counties. He writes serious and humorous short stories, novellas, and plays.

Onie Grosshans got her first library card at the age of eight, bicycling every two weeks to return read books for new ones to devour. Reading opened up new worlds for her, much needed at the time. She has continued to be a reader, mostly history, but moved into fiction in hopes of becoming a better writer. In the meantime, Onie got herself educated: BS degree, Fort Hays State, Kansas; doctorate, Indiana University; four years on faculty at Ohio State, 31 years at the University of Utah; now retired. Writing is complex, but Onie has enjoyed the challenge, even though much of her work is rejected—for good reason—but she is learning why and making corrections.

After a U of Chicago AB, **Albert Howard Carter, III,** went to U of Iowa for an MA in English and a PhD in Comparative Lit, with courses in the Writers' Workshop. He taught at Eckerd College, St. Petersburg, FL, for many years, then was adjunct professor in Social Medicine, School of Medicine, University of North Carolina–Chapel Hill. He trained as an EMT and served as a pastoral care visitor in hospitals, also a music visitor to patients. His nonfiction books include *First Cut: A Season in the Human Anatomy Lab*, *Our Human Hearts: A Medical and Cultural Journey*, and *Clowns and Jokers Can Heal Us: Comedy and Medicine*. His prose and poems have appeared in *New England Journal of Medicine*, *JAMA*, *Hiram Review*, *Ars Medica*, *Blood and Thunder*, *The Thomas Wolfe Review*, and *The Twin Bill*.

Becky Jensen is an author, freelance writer, and podcast contributor who lives and works in a little cabin on a wild river in northern Colorado. In addition to her debut memoir *No Man's Land: Unpacking One Woman's Worth on the Colorado Trail*, she wrote the lead story in *Rise: An Anthology of Change*, winner of the Colorado Book Award. When she's not hiking in the mountains, she's working on her next book about moving in with her mom (who has Alzheimer's) during ten weeks of wildfire evacuation. You can find her at beckyjensenwrites.com.

Made in the USA
Coppell, TX
16 January 2026